TALES OF THE 21ST CENTURY

MARGARET SIMS

Contents

Anatomy of Frustration

September 2023

Synopsis

Standardised protocols may appear on the surface to be efficient but most consumers find them incredibly frustrating. This play is based on my own experience (apart from the ending as I am clearly still here to tell the story!).

Characters

- **PERSON 1**: Any age and gender (Mary/Marty)

- **PERSON 2**: Plays a range of different roles – any age or gender

PERSON 2: You're sitting in a tree?

PERSON 1: Yep, I am.

PERSON 2: Mind telling me why?

PERSON 1: Sure, okay. It all started when a warning light came on in my car.

PERSON 2: Your what?

PERSON 1: Yeah, and I guess I was lucky because I can now get it serviced in Tamworth instead of going to Sydney. So, I called them up and booked it in.

PERSON 2: Okay, and then?

PERSON 1: I went down, and they couldn't find anything wrong with it. They said they just reset it, and that was it.

PERSON 2: Right.

PERSON 1: So it was fine for a while, and then it came on again, so I booked it in and took it down. They said perhaps the sensor was faulty, but of course, they didn't have one in stock, so I had to take it back for a third time for them to replace it.

PERSON 2: Okay.

PERSON 1: It was fine for a while, and then it came on again, so I booked it in. I went down really early because it was a Friday, and I needed to go away the following weekend. After about an hour and a half, some guy – I'm assuming the service manager – came to me and said he had good news and bad news.

PERSON 2: And?

PERSON 1: They didn't know what was wrong with it but figured it must've been something, seeing as this was such a consistent problem. So, they were going to need a lot more time. The good news was that, since it was a warranty job, they could organize a hire car for me. They had booked the job with the head office and lodged the request for a hire car, and the head office would get in touch with me at some point. He then asked me if I wanted to go home and wait for the call. I pointed out that I was 120 km from home, and there was no public transport, so I would have to wait for the call in their waiting room. So, they left me there, and I waited. About two hours later, the same guy came and asked if I was still there, and of course I was, so he gave me the number to call them up myself. So, I did.

(Lights fade and come back up. PERSON 2 is now the assistant on the phone – as the role changes, there can be a minimal costume change)

PERSON 2: You have reached customer care. Press 1 for Roadside Assistance, press 2 for Customer Care, press 3 for Sales.

PERSON 1: I didn't know which to press, so I thought for a minute.

PERSON 2: No response has been received. Goodbye.

PERSON 1: I rang them again.

PERSON 2: You have reached customer care. Press 1 for Roadside Assistance, press 2 for Customer Care, press 3 for Sales.

PERSON 1: I took a stab in the dark and pressed 2 for Customer Care.

PERSON 2: You have reached customer care. Press 1 for New Inquiries, press 2 for Existing Inquiries.

PERSON 1: Well, the service guy had given me a job number, so I pressed 2.

PERSON 2: Please enter your job number.

PERSON 1: So I did.

PERSON 2: Your job number is XJ534792. Press 1 if this is correct, press 2 if this is incorrect.

PERSON 1: I pressed 1.

PERSON 2: You are 10th in the queue. Please hold.

PERSON 1: The annoying music played for a while.

PERSON 2: You are now 9th in the queue. If you would like to receive a callback, press 1 now, followed by the hash key.

PERSON 1: I pressed 1.

PERSON 2: Your callback request has been recorded. Goodbye

PERSON 1: So I waited. About half an hour later, I got a call.

PERSON 2: This is your Customer Care callback. Please enter your job number followed by the hash key

PERSON 1: I entered my job number… *(pause)*

PERSON 2: No response has been received. Goodbye.

PERSON 1: I swore in frustration and called the main number again

PERSON 2: You have reached Customer Care. Press 1 for Roadside Assistance, press 2 for Customer Care, press 3 for Sales.

PERSON 1: I pressed 2

PERSON 2: You have reached Customer Care. Press 1 for New Inquiries, press 2 for Existing Inquiries.

PERSON 1: I pressed 2.

PERSON 2: Please enter your job number.

PERSON 1: So I did.

PERSON 2: Your job number is XJ534792. Press 1 if this is correct, press 2 if this is incorrect.

PERSON 1: I pressed 1.

PERSON 2: You are now 8th in the queue. If you would like to receive a callback, press 1 now, followed by the hash key.

PERSON 1: I pressed 1#.

PERSON 2: Your callback request has been recorded. Goodbye.

PERSON 1: So I wait, and I wait, and I wait. I go and get some lunch, and I come back and I wait. Then I get a call.

PERSON 2: This is your Customer Care callback. Please enter your job number, followed by the hash key

PERSON 1: I cross my fingers and enter the job number. I hear it clicking through.

PERSON 2: You have reached Jess/Josh. How can I help you?

PERSON 1: Hello Jess/Josh, my name is Mary/Marty, and the job number is XJ534792. I am sitting in Tamworth, 120 km from home, waiting to hear back about a rental car replacement for the warranty job needed on my car.

PERSON 2: Please give me a moment, and I will look it up for you.

PERSON 1: Thank you. *(a pause; we can hear the tapping of computer keys)*.

PERSON 2: Yes, I see the job has been lodged, and the request for a rental car has been placed in the system. Is there anything else I can do for you?

PERSON 1: Can you please tell me how long it is going to take before I hear about the rental car?

PERSON 2: I'm sorry, but I cannot say anything. It has been lodged in the system and needs approval from our manager.

PERSON 1: Please understand I am 120 km away from home with no way of getting home without the car. It is now Friday afternoon, and if this doesn't get sorted soon, I will be stranded. Can you please find out how long it will take to get the rental car approved?

PERSON 2: I am sorry. It has been passed through our system and is now at the next level for approval.

PERSON 1: Could you please give me the contact name and number of the person who needs to approve it so I can talk to them directly?

PERSON 2: I'm afraid I cannot do that. It is an internal number.

PERSON 1: Can you please pass me on to your supervisor?

PERSON 2: One moment, please. I will check.

PERSON 1: So I wait.

PERSON 2: I am sorry, my supervisor is on another call. Can I get him to call you back?

PERSON 1: Thank you, that would be good. Please understand that this is now urgent.

PERSON 2: I will pass on the request. Goodbye.

PERSON 1: So I wait, and I finally get a call.

PERSON 2: This is the Customer Care service manager. How can I help you?

PERSON 1: My name is Mary/Marty, and the job number is XJ534792.

PERSON 2: One moment, please, while I look it up. (pause) Ah yes, I have it in front of me.

PERSON 1: Great. Please understand that I am now sitting 120 km from home in Tamworth. There is no public transport. There is no other way of getting home apart from having a replacement car. Can you please tell me when approval for this will come through?

PERSON 2: I am sorry, but these approvals can often take three or four days.

PERSON 1: Three or four days is not possible. Please understand that I have no way of getting home, and 120 km is a very long way to walk.

PERSON 2: It is in the system. You will need to wait.

PERSON 1: Please understand that waiting is not feasible. This place will close very soon for the weekend, and I have no way of getting home. I have nowhere to go. The replacement car is urgent.

PERSON 2: How you get home is not our responsibility. Your request is in the system and will be processed in due time.

PERSON 1: This is not acceptable. I am stranded. I have nowhere to go and no way to get home!

PERSON 2: This is not our responsibility. Your request is in the system.

PERSON 1: Can you please give me the contact details of the person with whom the request is now sitting?

PERSON 2: I'm afraid I cannot do that. It is an internal number.

PERSON 1: There must be some way I can contact that person. Can you please give me the information I need to follow this request up?

PERSON 2: I'm afraid I cannot do that. It is an internal number. Goodbye.

PERSON 1: I scream in frustration and start figuring out my options. I could call my family, but it is a long way to come all the way down to Tamworth to collect me and take me back. I wonder if I can get a seat on the train as it comes through Tamworth on its way to Armidale, but when I check, it is already too late. And then I get a call.

PERSON 2: This is Roadside Assistance. We have received a request for a replacement rental car for you. This is a courtesy call to let you know that we are currently trying to find one available in your area. We will get back to you as soon as possible.

PERSON 1: Thank you so much. I really appreciate it. Do you think you will be able to find one before the close of business today? Because I am 120 km from home with no way of getting there

PERSON 2: No, I cannot say. We do not know what cars are available in your area. Please wait, and we will get back to you as soon as possible.

PERSON 1: I cross my fingers and hope because, at this point, I've missed the train, and I'm pretty much done for. And around 4:30, I get a call.

PERSON 2: We have a rental car available for you. Please call this number and give them your name – they are expecting your call.

PERSON 1: So I do, and yes, they have a booking for me. That's wonderful, thank you very much. Now, I'm at the dealer's business location. Could you please come and pick me up as I do not have a way to get to you?

PERSON 2: I'm sorry, we don't have the staff available to do that. You will need to make your way to us.

PERSON 1: It's on the other side of town, but luckily, the nice service manager arranged for someone to drop me off – I guess they wanted me out of their waiting room before they closed – after all, I have been there since 7:45 a.m. I do a last-minute grab of things from my car that I think I might need, pick up the rental car, and start making my way home. And wouldn't you know it, halfway up the Moonbies, the car stops. I swear, and I look in the glovebox to find the emergency assistance number, and I ring it.

PERSON 2: Emergency Assistance, how can I help you?

PERSON 1: It's Mary/Marty here. I have a rental car and it has broken down halfway up the Moonbies.

PERSON 2: We do not have any roadside assistance available at this point. I will lodge your request and get someone to reach out to you as soon as possible.

PERSON 1: Do you have any idea how long this might take?

PERSON 2: Well, I cannot say, but I suspect several hours.

PERSON 1: It's getting dark, and I am stopped in the inside lane, just around a corner, where there is nowhere for me to go back and get off the road. There is no verge where I am. I think where I am stopped is quite dangerous, but I didn't have a choice. The car stopped, not me.

PERSON 2: Can you not push the car forward until you reach a stopping bay?

PERSON 1: I am driving up the Moonbies. It is a very steep hill. I am not strong enough to push a car up a hill.

PERSON 2: You will need to put your flashing lights on and place your emergency cone behind the car.

PERSON 1: The indicators don't work. Nothing is working, but I will look in the boot to see if there is an emergency cone. So I look, but there is nothing in the car - no roadside emergency kit or anything, so I tell them that.

PERSON 2: You will need to stand behind your car with a torch as it gets dark.

PERSON 1: I don't have a torch in the car. This is not my car. It is a rental car, and the battery on my phone is getting flat. It will not last long, and there is nowhere here to charge it.

PERSON 2: We will get someone to you as soon as possible, but it will take some time.

PERSON 1: So I stand behind the car with the phone in my hand, keeping my fingers crossed. A few cars go by, but no one stops, of course. It gets dark, and it's starting to get cold, and of course, I haven't bought anything warm. Then I hear the sound of a car coming really, really fast and a siren following it. I fumble with my phone to turn the torch on to indicate that I am standing there and my car is just around the corner. There's a flash of headlights, a massive crash, then a second crash, and an enormous explosion. And now I'm sitting here in the tree.

PERSON 2: You do know you are dead, don't you?

PERSON 1: Well, I had figured that out, considering I haven't been able to climb trees for years.

PERSON 2: Okay, so we need to sort out where you go next. What religion are you?

PERSON 1: I'm not religious.

PERSON 2: Oh, an agnostic. You know, I'm not sure what we should do with you. I'm new at this job. Hang on a minute, and I'll get back to you. *(Person 2 exits)*

PERSON 1: I wait - not sure how long. Time kind of doesn't have any meaning anymore.

PERSON 2: *(Person 2 enters)* Right, so I talked to my boss, and it appears that for agnostics, we need you to complete this survey. I have a copy here. Question one: Tell me how you died.

PERSON 1: Oh, for God's sake.

PERSON 2: We do accept customer abuse. Goodbye.

(Lights dim. There's a sound of falling and a crash, and the lights come up red, ideally flashing red.)

PERSON 2: Welcome to Hell. Please enter your customer number.

PERSON 1: I have no idea what my customer number is.

PERSON 2: No number has been recorded. Goodbye.

PERSON 1: *(a screaming tantrum – lights down)*

THE END

Baby Talk

June 2024

Synopsis

There is growing recognition that babies can communicate from the moment of birth as long as we take the time to observe and learn their signals. However, most adults are oblivious to this rich communication. What would babies say about us if they had the words?

Characters

- **LULUBELLE** - Female baby

- **SNOOKINS** - Male or female baby

- **JOSIE** - Lulubelle's mother

- **MEGAN** - Snookins' mother

Actors playing Lulubelle and Snookins should be older than the actors playing the mothers.

Lulubelle and Snookins are sitting on the floor with a few toys scattered around them - their backs are to the chairs where their mothers are sitting. Josie is sitting in a chair. Throughout the play, when the babies are talking to each other, they have their backs to their mothers.

Megan enters carrying two glasses of wine, hands one to Josie and throws herself into her chair.

MEGAN: Here you go, Josie. I need this a damn sight more than I need a coffee.

JOSIE: Lovely, thanks, but I think there's a risk this will put me to sleep.

MEGAN: Lulubelle is still not sleeping through the night?

Lulubelle turns and looks at her mother and smiles.

LULUBELLE: Goo goo gaga

Lulubelle turns her back to her mother

LULUBELLE: Ha! Sleeping! You gotta be kidding. Nighttime is interesting.

SNOOKINS: What do you mean?

LULUBELLE: It's just me and her time. None of the other Demons they call my siblings are around, and I get her all to myself.

JOSIE: No. I thought we had this sleeping thing controlled, but recently, she's been waking up several times a night, and I really struggle to get her to go back to sleep.

MEGAN: Perhaps you ought to try what I do.

JOSIE: What's that?

MEGAN: Snookins was a horror to get to sleep, so I did the controlled crying programme.

JOSIE: I don't think I could stand listening to her cry herself to sleep.

MEGAN: You've got to figure out what is more important - your sanity or pandering to her every whim.

Snookins looks at Megan

SNOOKINS: Goo goo gaga goo

SNOOKINS turns back to Megan and gives the fingers.

SNOOKINS: I quickly figured out the Mobile Cow wasn't going to come to me, but I get my revenge.

LULUBELLE: How?

SNOOKINS: You ought to smell the nappy that I present her with when she doesn't come to me at night. It's toxic.

LULUBELLE: (*sniggers*) That's smart.

JOSIE: I don't know. I'm hoping she will eventually feel sufficiently secure to be able to put herself back to sleep when she wakes.

LULUBELLE: And what did I hear you call your mother?

SNOOKINS: I call the Walking Milk Factory lots of names.

LULUBELLE: (*giggles*) That's funny.

SNOOKINS: Well, I have to amuse myself somehow. Just because my stupid hands don't work well enough yet to do something decent with these crappy toys doesn't mean my brain should atrophy.

Snookins waves hands about and sends a couple of toys flying.

LULUBELLE: I can't wait until I can crawl. The other monsters in my house of horrors leave their stuff all over the place. A wonderful invitation for a curious baby.

MEGAN: How are you going with a solid food thing?

JOSIE: Okay, I guess. The books all say just introduce one food at a time to check for allergies but none of my other kids are allergic. I suspect I went overboard with the first; I was so careful. The second child, I was a little more relaxed, and with LULUBELLE, I've been really slack.

MEGAN: I had all the best intentions in the world. I was planning to prepare only organic foods and limit sugar intake, but it does get to be a real drag.

JOSIE: Yes, I know and you don't want to get into the habit of cooking different foods for different family members. You could go insane.

MEGAN: Luckily, it's only me, my partner and Snookins.

JOSIE: You're not planning on another?

MEGAN: God, no! I don't know how you cope with a houseful.

LULUBELLE looks at her mother.

LULUBELLE: Goo goo gaga.

JOSIE: When she looks at me as if I'm everything in her world, my heart just melts.

LULUBELLE turns away with her back to her mother again.

LULUBELLE: Everything in my world! Ha! Dream on! I've got her completely under my thumb. One look and I pretty much get what I want.

SNOOKINS: I'm not sure how you manage that. She has to divide her attention amongst the three of you.

LULUBELLE: My Demon brother and sister, you mean? Nah. The cuteness gets them all, every time.

SNOOKINS: (*sniggers*) You mean the big, wide-eyed innocent look.

SNOOKINS models the look, turns to the 2 mothers and shows them.

JOSIE and MEGAN: Aww!

SNOOKINS turns back.

LULUBELLE: Absolutely.

MEGAN: I don't care how cute the little poo bags are. One is enough for me.

Snookins looks at Megan

SNOOKINS: Goo goo gaga goo

Snookins turns back.

SNOOKINS: Thank God for that! I have enough trouble getting her attention. I can't imagine competing with other Demons.

LULUBELLE: It's not that bad, and anyway, the big eyes work with the other Demons as well as Mum. There's always someone who will come running when I cry.

JOSIE: So, when are you thinking you might go back to work?

MEGAN: My maternity leave is just about up. I have a place for Snookins in the childcare centre down the road. The plan is to be back full-time in the next three months, but I will start part-time.

JOSIE: Are you looking forward to going back?

MEGAN: I'd kill sometimes for adult conversation.

JOSIE: I know what you mean

MEGAN: Derek's been working extra shifts while I've been on leave, and when he gets home, he's so tired. All he wants to do is flop. All I crave is some adult conversation, but most of the time, he's fallen asleep before I can even start.

JOSIE: I'm with you there. How does he cope with Snookins?

MEGAN: He doesn't do much - says he's too tired when he gets home. Really, he's not very good with Snookins at all.

JOSIE: Sometimes I wish Peter would leave the kids alone. He comes home from work and makes such a big fuss of all the kids. He winds them up with rough and tumble play, and someone always ends up crying.

Lulubelle looks at her mother.

LULUBELLE: Goo gaga.

Lulubelle turns back.

LULUBELLE: It's sacks on Dad when he comes home. The other Demons jump up and down all over him, and he rolls around the floor with them. And sometimes the Demons get me by mistake. I make a point of howling REALLY loudly.

SNOOKINS: It sounds like hell.

LULUBELLE: We all yell and scream and laugh but there's always crying as well. Mum says he doesn't know when to stop.

SNOOKINS: Yuk, yuk, yuk.

LULUBELLE: What's this about you going to childcare?

SNOOKINS: The Mobile Cow wants to go back to work. I'm quite looking forward to it, actually. I suspect there will be lots for me to do, but of course, I will have to yell and scream when the cow leaves me there. And yell and scream again when she comes to pick me up.

LULUBELLE: (*snickers*) Sounds like you have fun planned.

SNOOKINS: Absolutely. Are you going to go to childcare?

LULUBELLE: I'm not sure.

MEGAN: I don't know which is worse. A dad who doesn't play with the kid or one who doesn't know when to stop playing with the kid.

JOSIE: You're right. The other two start school next year, so I'm thinking I might try finding a part-time job and putting Lulubelle in childcare.

SNOOKINS: Hey, there's your answer. Next year. Hope your mum puts you with me.

LULUBELLE: That would be great. Once they both start working, we won't have time to catch up.

SNOOKINS: Oh, my god. That will be awful.

Snookins begins to cry loudly.

Lulubelle watches for a moment and then begins to cry as well.

JOSIE: What happened? What set them off?

MEGAN: I have absolutely no idea.

JOSIE: Perhaps it's time for Lulubelle's nap. I'd better get going. Thanks for a lovely play date.

Josie gathers up the toys and pretends to pick up Lulubelle. The actor playing Lulubelle stands up.

MEGAN: I'll see you next week, okay?

JOSIE: Yep, all good. Bye for now. Bye Snookins.

Josie waves in an exaggerated fashion at Snookins. Snookins sees Lulubelle going and reaches her arms out towards her and cries even more loudly. Lulubelle follows Josie out, still crying and appearing to struggle as if reaching back for Snookins.

When they are gone, Megan grabs the hands of the actor playing Snookins and pulls to stand.

MEGAN: Come on you. Clearly, you're tired. Let's put you down for a nap.

Megan exits with Snookins following. Just before disappearing, Snookins glances back at the audience, grins cheekily, and gives a thumbs-up gesture.

THE END

Bullshit

June 2017

Synopsis

The world of work is changing and, in particular, the way workers are perceived by management. Despite the empty rhetoric that positions workers as valuable assets, the experience of many workers is that they are disposable resources who can be exploited then discarded.

Characters

- **FINLEY** – male or female – late 20s through to 50s

- **LANDRY** – male or female – a little older than Finley

The Characters are not talking to each other throughout.

FINLEY: Look at the stars. Aren't they gorgeous tonight? I used to be a star once. Well, sort of star really. I remember when I first started working. Everything came so easily. Success after success. I felt like I was shining. Employee of the year in my very first year. The boss knew me by name and used to say hello when I saw him in the car park as we both headed to work early in the morning. We were often the first to arrive. I used to rush in and get started right away, didn't even stop for coffee. I felt like I could do anything – anything at all. And I loved the work. I couldn't wait to get to work in the morning and get going. It was so exciting. Sometimes, I didn't want to go home at the end of the day. I would think about work in the evenings, and sometimes I would even dream about it. You know, some of my best ideas came to me in dreams. The dreams were great – sort of like daydreams. I could try out new ideas and play with them night after night, trying different scenarios and trying to figure out any glitches. By the time I actually tried something at work, I had gone through it so many times in my head that it almost felt old-fashioned. Everyone said I was on my way up the career ladder. The future was rushing towards me with hands out in welcome. I had it all. I could see myself getting promotion after promotion. Everyone knew me and knew I was on the fast track. People would come to me for ideas, and would ask my opinion. I learned so much about all parts of the organisation when I talked to so many different people, and helped them.

People would greet me outside work, in the supermarket, and on the street. Everyone seemed so happy and secure in what they were doing. It's sort of a cliché, I guess, but I really felt like I was part of a big, happy family. My life was great.

But I suppose the good times can't last forever. It was such a slow change I didn't really realise what was happening for ages. Perhaps the first sign was when I didn't get the supervisor position I was expecting. I sort of blamed myself at the time. I had taken it for granted. I was really busy with something; I can't remember now what it was, but I was really engrossed, and I kind of whipped up an application really quickly. I figured everyone knew me, and it was just to satisfy protocol that I had to apply. It was such a shock when they told me I didn't have the position. I was kind of dazed and didn't quite believe it. Then I told myself I didn't really want the position cause it would take me away from what I really enjoyed doing. So, I carried on doing what I loved. And Landry came along. Yes, it was Landry who got the position and became my boss. I really liked him/her in those early days. S/he spent time with all of us and got to know what we were doing. I thought that was great. Especially as s/he did not have the same background as the rest of us. Landry was management trained and couldn't do what we do if his/her life depended on it. S/he even came out to the pub with us a couple of times. I figured all was well.

Then, I don't know if Landry changed, or if the nicey nice face s/he started with had been a pretence, but things started to change. I remember one meeting, Landry called us all together and told us …

LANDRY: We need to be more efficient to survive in this modern world. The way things have been in the past is not good enough. We need to improve our output, work more efficiently. You all need to work more efficiently. And I am going to make some changes to how things operate around here so you can all be more efficient. Right. First up ….

FINLEY: And I guess that was the start. Landry's idea of efficiency was to standardise what we do. Follow the process every time, all the time, and according to Landry, we will be more efficient. Well, that didn't work for me. I've always done things my way, and things got done, often faster than others, and they got done well. After all, that was my reputation and everyone knew that. At first, I kind of figured that these rules were not important, or at least they were not for me. After all, I had the best output of everyone. Why would anyone want to mess with that? I thought that perhaps they would apply to those who were not doing so well, but not to me. I soon learned.

LANDRY: Finley, I see that you have submitted your work for last week but I do not see Form 56A. Unless you submit Form 56A with your work, we cannot accept that you have done your work for the week.

FINLEY: Form 56A. A nightmare. In the beginning, it used to take me at least 2 hours a day to fill in the form for the day's work. That's 2 hours EVERY DAY. 2 hours filling in a form reporting what I had done. I could have spent those 2 hours doing another 20% more work. But no, I have to fill in the form. Every damn day.

LANDRY: Finley, I have been looking through your Form 56As for the last few weeks. I see that you have not completed Section 76 in any of them. I expect to have the corrected forms on my desk before COB today. Form 56A shows head office we are doing our jobs in this division. We are all accountable to others for what we do, and you are letting the rest of the division down. And you know how important it is that we deliver quality outputs.

FINLEY: Section 76. Oh yes, Section 76. How many hours and minutes have I spent on each element of my work. Each element has a drop-down box, and you have to select the relevant time. As we are supposed to work 7.5 hours a day, it does not allow you to claim any more than that. But that doesn't allow for the times I work through lunch, or take a task home in the evening, or when I come in at the weekend to follow up on something that I'm working on. So I lie. I make a rough guess and forget it.

LANDRY: Finley, I see in Section 76 you have claimed several hours each day last week on Task 11c. I specifically assigned that to Brigid. I asked Brigid if she had asked for your help and she said she had not. Explain.

FINLEY: Explain? Explain! What the fuck was Task 11c? I had no idea so had to search through the procedures manual to find it. Oh yeah, that. Well, I had been doing some of that, but not for the specific task Brigid was working on. I was playing with a new idea for something, but it was not clear in my head yet, so I didn't want to pass that one on to Landry. If it worked, the bastard would claim it to be his/her idea. If it didn't, I'd get bitched at for wasting time. Anyway, I made up some kind of bullshit story and didn't hear any more about it. Well, not directly, anyway. Not long after that, there was a staff meeting. I hate those things. We all sit in a room together and get talked at – much of the stuff could have been shared with us via email, though, to be honest, I am not sure how many would bother to read it. It's all such bullshit. And I swear Landry was having a dig at me.

LANDRY: I am sure you will all agree that teamwork is so important. When we all work together, the synergy from our co-operation improves our outputs. The processes I have developed are to guide our teamwork. When we each do our part of the process correctly, together, we create a synergy that improves our organisation. It is so important that we all follow the processes laid down. That way, you know that you are doing your best work, and I know that you are doing your fair share. There is no room for mavericks. We must all work together, support each other. I am sure you all agree that quality is important and quality is best achieved when we all follow the processes laid down.

FINLEY: And then Landry moved up the hierarchy and Darby moved into the supervisor role. Darby used to work with us, and we all figured he would be a great supervisor. He knew the realities of our day-to-day work. Not like Landry. I even thought there might be a chance to change the dreaded Form 56A and get something that was easier to complete, a better reflection of what we actually do. How wrong I was. Darby seemed to change overnight. He would say nice, supportive things to my face, but nothing ever changed. No changes to Form 56A, nothing got better, in fact things got worse. Darby would not make a decision, ever. He kept saying it was not in his authority or that he had to confer with Landry. Or he would say he'd look into it, but nothing ever happened, and he never got back with an answer. I remember once taking an idea to him for a new development. He refused to have anything to do with the idea and insisted I attend a meeting with him and Landry to explore the idea.

LANDRY: I am disappointed in you, Finley. You waste my time with this half-baked idea. If you want to suggest a new development then you need to support that with a full business plan. Where is the expertise in the team to undertake this? What are the implications for staffing? What percentage of the market share is this likely to generate? Now I know Darby is in the middle of developing a staffing plan and a business plan for the Division. That is exactly the kind of work I expect if we are to consider any changes to the division.

FINLEY: Darby sat there, mum, and said nothing, not a bloody thing. Didn't explain that he had insisted on the meeting before allowing any preliminary discussion of my idea. Didn't explain that he had not told me I needed to do a full business plan before having even a preliminary discussion. Didn't explain that this was intended to simply be an exploratory discussion. Basically, dropped me in it up to my ears and sat there smirking whilst he was praised. I came out of that meeting fuming, absolutely furious. What a gutless prick. And, you know, I never saw that division business and staffing plan Mr Wonderful was supposed to be writing. Maybe Darby developed it and never showed us workers. Wouldn't surprise me. If he did, I wonder what was in it.

And then came the cuts. Suddenly, we seemed to be chronically short of money. There was a staffing freeze. No new positions, and when people left, they were not replaced. Unless they were managers of course – there seemed to be no problem replacing them. Darby left and was replaced by John. John didn't stay long and was replaced by Alex. But over that time, not one of the workers was replaced. My team went from 20 people to 12. The work did not decrease, we all just had to somehow manage to get through it all. Most nights, I found myself doing 2-3 hours extra just to get through it, and filling in Form 56A made me mad. It still would not allow me to claim more than 7.5 hours a day, so the whole thing was just reporting lies. And I got into constant trouble because what I reported on Form 56A was not my reality, and Alex was on my back all the time, telling me I was not spending enough time on each of the tasks

I needed to do. I don't know what I was supposed to do. Take longer to do the work and not finish each day? Perhaps, looking back, that is what I should have done. Getting through all the extra work every day simply sent a message that this volume of work was okay. And it was not. I could see colleagues around me getting more and more stressed, and people were going off sick all the time. That made things worse as their work had to be covered while they were off. People stopped interacting; they would lock themselves away and work and not talk to each other anymore. No one went to morning tea and lunch. Everyone was head down, working, working, working. We stopped going to the pub on Friday nights. People just wanted to get out of the place and forget it for the weekend. I started feeling sick when I went to work each day. I started arriving on time instead of early. For the first time in my working life, I began using my sick leave. Sometimes, just having a day off was all that stood between me and total insanity. And, you know, what used to really raise my blood pressure was the bullshit way the bosses talked about things. It was just so artificial and so not my reality.

LANDRY: I am sure you will all join with me in congratulating Alex. The division is the best-performing division in the organisation. You can all be so proud that you are creating the highest quality output, one which is highly valued by clients. In recognition of Alex's hard work, he is being transferred to head office. Replacing him is Joel, who is coming to you from the southern division. Please welcome Joel, and I am confident he will keep up the hard work.

FINLEY: Congratulate Alex! It was not Alex who did the work, it was us. We could have done even better if he had not been wasting our time with that stupid Form 56A and his stupid staff meetings every fortnight. And Joel. Well, I am sure the southern division danced for joy when he left them. Within weeks, he had 'improved' Form 56A. He had us clocking in and out and not only yelled at us if we did overtime but yelled at us if we did not complete the work as well. There was no way we could do the work and NOT do overtime, so we were always in trouble. I heard him tell Sam, down the corridor, that he was a useless piece of shit and if he didn't pull his finger out, he (Joel) would make sure he was sacked. He refused to let Jan take one day of annual leave the Thursday before

Easter so she could go away with her family. He made Sergei get a medical certificate for every day of sick leave taken because he said Sergei had taken too many sick days and, therefore, could not be trusted. Brigid resigned. She had been working on a project that Alex had set her for months. She'd put her heart and soul into it and was really pleased with what she had done. Joel told her it was a complete waste of time and money and that he was putting her on an official warning as she had not met her work targets over the months she had been working on the project. It destroyed her. Most of the team began looking for other jobs.

I could see people collapsing all around me. Confident, efficient colleagues became haunted shells, too scared to say boo. And then Joel started on me. I had not filled in Form 56A correctly – week after week, it would come back with red lines through different parts, and I would have to redo it. I used to copy and paste from the week before, and each week, something that had been okay the previous week was now suddenly not okay this week. It drove me nuts. I started spending more time on Form 56A than I did on my bloody work. I stopped caring about what I was doing. Just did what I had to and no more. Work became a nightmare. I felt trapped but couldn't see a way out. I started questioning myself – perhaps I was not suited for this work. But if not this, then what? Had I wasted my life doing this when perhaps there was something else out there I could have been doing? Then Joel got an assistant - we were still terribly short-staffed, of course, but clearly Joel needed help drawing his red lines through Form 56A. Not long after, I got an email from Landry demanding I have a meeting with him. I asked what it was about, and he simply said:

LANDRY: I want to have an informal discussion about the division and your performance in it.

FINLEY: I thought – oh shit – and got my union to provide a support person to go with me to the meeting. As per procedure, I informed Landry that Claire would be coming with me. I was feeling a bit guilty because I knew my work was not as good now as it had been in the past. It was hard to really care about it anymore. We rocked up to the meeting and – lo and behold – there sits Alison, the HR person from head office. Double shit! Landry launches into a whole pile of complaints Joel has lodged against me. Claire points out that Joel has not discussed any of these with me. Landry counters with a claim that Joel's red lines through my weekly Form 56As are sufficient evidence to prove my incompetence. He then goes on to claim that not only is there a problem with my Form 56A, but there is also a problem with me following due process. It appears that since Joel now has an assistant, the Form 56As should go to the assistant, not to Joel. At this point, I speak up and say that Joel has not informed the Division of this change in process, so it is unreasonable to expect us to know about it. Landry pays me no attention whatsoever, and goes on to say that it is clear I am not happy in my job and that he wants me to think about my future. He schedules another meeting tomorrow where we can follow up after I have had time to think and almost throws us out of the room.

Think about my future – we all know what that means. Resign or be sacked. Claire's advice is not to resign – she claims there are major breaches of process, and we can lodge a claim against them, but this will take time. We meet again the next day. Claire tells Landry that this process is illegal – against our enterprise agreement. Landry says he doesn't care and sacks me. He organises for me to be escorted immediately off the premises with the security guard picking up my bag and keys from my former office, so I can't even go back there to say goodbye to colleagues. Claire tells me that as I am no longer employed, the union cannot support me. She says I need to go to a lawyer as there is sufficient evidence to show that this process is illegal. However, when I try to get into my files, I find I can't. My work profile is locked, and all the evidence I need to prove I have been treated illegally is not accessible. I go to a lawyer and am told that without evidence, it is only my word against theirs. I can try if I want, but there is no guarantee of success, and it would cost me a lot of money. So here I am. Unemployed. No reference from my previous position. Enough money to last me a few weeks. Very few friends – I lost them all when I was working such long hours. Work colleagues too frightened to be seen with me in case they get targeted. And I wonder what I am good for. What can I do with my life now? What do I want to do? I really don't know. So much of my time was focused on work. There is nothing else. No family. No friends, and when my money runs out, no home. Probably unemployable. Who is going to give a job to someone my age with no references? It's so obvious on a CV – years and years working in one place and no reference from that place.

So, I'm sitting on the bridge, swinging my legs over the edge and looking at the stars. They really are beautiful tonight.

THE END

Customer loyalty

September 2024

Synopsis

When I was younger there was enormous benefit to demonstrating customer loyalty: long-term customers were rewarded with significant discounts. Now it appears that long-term customers are exploited by having their contracts switched to higher cost programmes at the end of a contract period, requiring them to check at each annual renewal to ensure they are getting the best deal.

Characters

- **MARCY**: female, any age

- **AGENT 1:** any gender, any age

- **AGENT 2:** any gender, any age. Can be played by the same person as Agent 1 with an indicative costume change

- **JO**: Marcy's partner – any gender

Start with a projection of a sign that says:

<u>Partnership Wizard</u>

Is your partner costing you too much?

We will compare partnership plans and organise the best deal for you.

Free service.

Marcy enters, talking to herself.

MARCY: Things have been a bit expensive lately. I suppose it wouldn't hurt to check, but I feel a bit guilty. Things are fine between us, so maybe change is not a good thing.

She rings the number. When it's answered, the light comes up on the other side of the stage to find a customer service agent speaking to her.

AGENT 1: Relationship Wizard. How can I help you?

MARCY: I've just seen your ad, and I think I should probably check my relationship plan.

AGENT 1: Certainly, madam. Can I have your name, address, and phone number, please?

MARCY: Marcy Fairchild, 97 Bracken, Way, Armidale, NSW 2350, 0432 167 985.

AGENT 1: Got it. Alright, can you tell me which plan you have at the moment?

MARCY: Just a minute, and I can pull it up on the phone.

She taps away and then speaks.

MARCY: The plan is with Partnerships Inc., and it's their Super Satisfaction Plan.

Agent taps on her computer for a moment and then speaks.

AGENT 1: Right, I can see your details now. Your plan expired some time ago, and they automatically transferred you to their more expensive Double Super Satisfaction plan. With this, you qualify for birthday and anniversary reminders along with suggestions for appropriate presents. Let me just run a comparison and see if I can come up with a better deal for you.

Agent taps on the computer.

AGENT 1: Right, I have a number of options available for you. The first is 'Relationships Guru' and looking at their policies, their basic relationships plan has the same benefits as your current plan and it would save you $1000 a month. For an extra $200 a month, you can add suggestions for appropriate love messaging to your partner; key words to keep your relationship fresh.

MARCY: Not sure I need that. I've been with my current partner for nearly 20 years now, and things are fine.

AGENT 1: Then we have 'Secure Relationships' whose Budget Relationship Plan has better benefits than your current plan. You can have birthday, Christmas, and anniversary presents purchased on your behalf for your partner. Finally, we have 'Relationships r'us.' Their Saver Plan has the same benefits as your current plan, and for an additional $500 a month, they will organise an annual romantic getaway for you and your partner.

MARCY: What are the catches with these plans?

AGENT 1: All have an annual increase in fees and a standard contract period of 3 years. After 3 years you are transferred into a higher level, more expensive plan.

MARCY: Is that the same for all of them?

AGENT 1: Yes. Most of these firms rely on customers, not bothering to check their plans so that annual increments and fees are not noticed.

MARCY: I'm not sure.

AGENT 1: If you change to any of these other agencies, you will save between $500 and $1000 a month.

MARCY: Doesn't the auspicing agency pay my partner to stay in our relationship? And if my payments are decreasing, surely my partner's will too.

AGENT 1: No. Your partner's been on a standard income all the time. The difference in fees is what the agency charges you for your partnership plan.

MARCY: So, all the increases I've been paying go to the agency, not my partner?

AGENT 1: That's right.

MARCY: Well, that's a rip-off. Changing seems like a good idea. But it's such a hassle.

AGENT 1: That is what we are here for.

MARCY: I guess so. But what about 'Partnerships Inc.,' my current agency? Don't they offer a better plan than what I have now? Can't I go back to my original plan with them?

AGENT 1: Absolutely not. Your original plan is only for new customers, not existing customers.

MARCY: That's crazy! Well, I guess common sense says I should go with the best savings. I don't care too much about all the extras.

AGENT 1: The best saving is with 'Relationships r'us'. Do you want the annual romantic getaway added to your plan?

MARCY: No, I don't think so. I have been with my partner for 20 years now, and things are fine as they are.

AGENT 1: Right. I'll email you a form to sign, and we can then organise that for you.

Lights Fade and come up with a different agent sitting at the desk.

Agent 2 makes a phone call. Marcy answers

AGENT 2: Am I speaking to Marcy Fairchild?

MARCY: Yes. Who is this, please?

AGENT 2: This is Frankie from 'Relationships, Inc.' I see that you have chosen to cancel your current relationship plan with us. Can we persuade you to remain with us?

Marcy: I have found a relationship plan that saves me $1000 a month, so unless you can match that I am not interested.

AGENT 2: $1000 a month. Let me have a look

There's a pause while the Agent taps on the computer.

AGENT 2: Ah, yes. We have just introduced the Committed Relationship Plan. This would save you $1200 a month. As part of this plan, we offer ideas for an individually planned romantic annual holiday for you and your partner, and we identify appropriate birthday, Christmas, and anniversary presents for you to give to your partner and show you where you can purchase these. For another $200 a month, we will send flowers to your partner from you every month with a suitably romantic note.

MARCY: But I was told that none of your plans were available to me as an existing customer.

AGENT 2: The sales team can only offer these discounts to new customers. I am in the retrieval team and we have the authority to offer these plans to keep your business.

MARCY: That's crazy.

AGENT 2: That is the system, Madame. Would you be interested in the Committed Relationship Plan?

MARCY: Yes.

AGENT 2: Your verbal consent is all I need. I will do the necessary paperwork and send you something to sign.

Marcy: But what about the plan I've signed up for with the other company?

AGENT 2: You don't need to worry about that. We will sort it out.

Lights fade and come up again

MARCY: I must make a note to check with 'Relationships Wizard' annually so that I can make sure I am on the cheapest plan.

Jo enters

JO: Hey Marcy.

They hug.

Jo: Hey, I've been looking at partnership plans and I think we can get a better deal. Things have got so expensive these days and I need a better income. There are plans that offer so much more – great holidays and all sorts of other things that would spice up our relationship. Things are getting a bit stale, don't you think? Let's contact 'Relationships Wizard' and see what we can get for me.

Lights fade.

THE END

Extension by Granny

May 2015

Synopsis

Students may not always understand the importance of the assignments they are required to complete in terms of the benefits for their learning. This is often reflected in their placing a low priority on the work required, leaving the academic responsible for marking their work to feel undervalued and disrespected.

Characters

PERSON A: any age/gender

PERSON B: any age/gender

PERSON C: any age/gender

PERSON A and PERSON B sitting in staffroom at morning tea

PERSON A: I'm not sure what to do. The student has asked for an extension. She says her son has been sick, and she didn't have time to work on the assignment.

PERSON B: Sounds reasonable to me. Happens all the time.

PERSON A: Yes, I know. And part of me sympathises. But the other part says that she is nearly graduating, and when she is out in the real world, deadlines don't get extended. You make it or you don't.

PERSON B: Hmm – like those internal research grants due tomorrow. No extension. Get it in or miss out.

PERSON A: And getting the final marks in. There's a deadline, and if I have to stay up all night too bad, they still have to be in.

PERSON B: Sometimes, I wonder if we are too easy on the extensions. It's not really a real:world experience for them, is it? Extensions for any little excuse.

PERSON A: But the more we try to police it, the more imaginative they are with their excuses. I've had some good ones this semester.

PERSON B: Like?

PERSON A: Well, I got a call the other day – and this is week 10 of semester, right – so assignment 1 was due weeks ago, and assignment 2 this week. And this student hadn't handed in anything. So he rang and asked if he could hand both assignments in together. And I said no, it is too late to submit Assignment 1. And he asked does that mean I fail the unit. I said yes. He said it wasn't his fault because he'd been arrested, and they would not let him on the internet to submit his assignment.

PERSON B: I guess you could ask for the police record or something.

PERSON A: It turned out that he was arrested and held overnight, but that was weeks ago.

PERSON B: So why did an overnight stop him studying?

PERSON A: He said he was too "traumatised." (*traumatised can be said with air quotes*)

PERSON B: Well, he may have been, but he still should have contacted you weeks ago.

PERSON A: He hasn't been participating online either, so I told him to make a case to withdraw without penalty.

PERSON B: What was he arrested for?

PERSON A – I was kinda scared to ask. Anyway, I sent him to Student Central to sort.

PERSON B: Hmm – I had an interesting one this semester as well. She called me and asked if she could have an extension because she was in training for the Olympics. I thought yeah right – what shower do you think I came down in – but it turned out she really was and they are off in PERSON A training camp for a few weeks.

PERSON A: What fun.

PERSON C comes in and makes a drink

PERSON C: Well, another grandmother has bit the dust.

PERSON A: What?

PERSON C: Oh, come on. You know that great piece of research – Sam circulated it last semester, about grandparents.

PERSON B: No, I must have missed it.

PERSON C: I'll send you the website. It's a great study about how enrolment at university impacts on the life expectancy of grandparents.

PERSON A: Seriously?

PERSON C: But of course. There is a serious risk to grandparent longevity when a grandchild enrolls at uni. Statistically significant results. The conclusion was that students needed to either run away from home and not tell anyone in their family they were at uni, or they needed to lie to their family and tell them they had enlisted in the Foreign Legion or something until they finished. Otherwise, the risk to grandparents' lives is enormous. I think the average number of grandparents lost per student was around 6.

PERSON B: Hah, I've had a couple of dead grandparents this semester, for sure.

PERSON A: There certainly seem to be a lot of families with more than the standard set of 4 grandparents that's for real.

PERSON C: A sad comment on today's society.

PERSON B: I wonder if anyone here ever keeps a count of the number of grandparents each of our students loose? Perhaps we ought to have a grandparent register so we could check each time we get an extension request to see which number grandparent it is this time.

PERSON C: Not a bad idea. Perhaps we could put that suggestion to the Teaching and Learning Committee.

PERSON B: Oh, but we'd have to write a formal proposal, and I have too much marking to do.

PERSON A: Talking about a sad comment, did you get that email from that problematic student – you know the one we talked about the other day who is in both our units?

PERSON C: The one yesterday where he asked for a special exam because he has to go to his brother's 21st the night before the exam.

PERSON A: Yeah, that's the one. Do we go with that as a reasonable request?

PERSON C: Hell no. He can party to his heart's content, but he still needs to be here for the exam the next morning.

PERSON B: Are there circumstances when they can get a deferred exam?

PERSON C: Oh sure. All those students caught in the Queensland floods a few years ago were given lots of extensions and a special exam ages afterwards. Not only because they REALLY couldn't get here but many lost their computers, their books and study notes and everything.

PERSON B: Oh, of course – that must have been really difficult for them.

PERSON A: Yeah, we also gave extensions to those students who went up to help with the rescue and clean-up. Seemed only fair. Really messy as we had outstanding results all over the place. I think there's still a couple we are trying to tidy up.

PERSON C: Now me, I'm mean and nasty. A student emailed today and asked for an extension because her husband surprised her with a romantic weekend away from tomorrow. I told her that she should have been working on the assignment for the past week or so as it was due today so she didn't need an extension - she was not going away till tomorrow.

PERSON B: I bet she was not happy.

PERSON C: Probably not, but tough. She clearly was not going to get it in by today.

PERSON A: We do get some interesting ones. Last year, I had one who argued that she needed an extension because her assignment was due on the day of the full moon, and she could not work on that day.

PERSON B: She is probably right – but then can she work on any other day?

PERSON A: Maybe not, judging by what was handed in.

PERSON C: I had one last week who failed to hand in the second part of the assignment. When I returned her assignment as a fail, she emailed me, claiming it was my fault because I didn't tell her that she had not done the second part when she handed it in.

PERSON B: (*sarcastically*) Well, clearly, you are not looking after her properly.

PERSON A: Hmm – I got quite an abusive email from a student last semester. He had totally misread the assignment, and I had to fail him as he just didn't have anything in it that I could legitimately say addressed the learning outcomes. He got really angry and said he was an HD student so it must be my fault that he misunderstood the question.

PERSON C: Yes, it's funny how it's always our fault. The fact that the rest of the class understood and addressed the question is irrelevant of course.

PERSON B: Of course. Oh well, marking is calling. I'm wading through 100 papers. What fun. Not!

PERSON B leaves

PERSON A: What fun indeed. Makes me wish I had a grandmother so I could go to her funeral.

PERSON C: No such luck. Anyway, the papers would just stay on your desk waiting for you to get back.

PERSON A: That's true. I wonder how we could work it so that someone else did the marking.

PERSON C: I guess you would have to take sick leave or something – maybe unpaid leave. Compassionate leave is only 3 days, and they wouldn't do your marking if you are only away for that time. You'd have to be away for much longer.

PERSON A: Might be worth it. Imagine, no more assignments to mark – you could come back when the marking is done. And get paid for it. Maybe we'd better dig out our old grannies.

PERSON B comes back in, reading a letter, looking worried.

PERSON B: Oh dear. My granny is really sick. She's asking that I come and look after her for a while. I wonder if I could get sick leave to go to the UK and be with her. Goodness, I'll have to arrange for someone to cover for me here. I wonder who I can ask.

PERSON A and PERSON C throw their balled up serviettes at PERSON B and storm out – PERSON B is left alone, staring after them, looking puzzled.

THE END

Long way Down

October 2022

Synopsis

Learning to listen to more than the words spoken is a skill absolutely essential for those working in the community sector, in education and health and any other profession involving working with people. This is not an easy skill to learn but failing to do so can have significant consequences.

Characters

- **PAT** – any age, male or female. A social worker, working for the Police

- **MAL** – any age, male or female

- **NICOLA** – female, late 20s through to 40s

Pat is sitting with legs hanging over a bridge or a tall building. Mal wanders across the bridge, sees Pat, and comes to sit beside him/her

MAL: Long way down.

PAT: ………. Yeeeah ………. I guess.

MAL: ……………….. gonna jump?

PAT: No (quickly, then a long pause) ………. Yeah …………. Maybe.

MAL: Hmmm …………. Wanna talk about it?

PAT: ……………………….. I made a mistake …………… a mistake ……………….really, just a mistake.

MAL: Hmmmmmmm ……………

Lights dim; Pat gets up, puts on a jacket, and sits at a desk working on a computer. Mal scoots to stage right and stays sitting out of the light

A knock on the door, and Nicola enters

NICOLA: (nervously, hesitantly) Excuse me. Your colleague told me to come here. Are you the social worker?

PAT: (Briskly) I'll be with you in a minute. Have a seat.

NICOLA sits and nervously twists her hands. After a minute, Pat finishes what s/he is doing and looks up

PAT: name

NICOLA: N--N--NICOLA.

PAT: Right, Nicola who?

NICOLA: Nicola Pearson.

PAT: Nicola Pearson (*types into the laptop*) Address?

NICOLA: 15 Longtree Lane.

PAT: Longtree Lane. Here in town?

NICOLA: Yes.

PAT: Okay, got it. How can I help you?

NICOLA: I don't know …… I'm not sure.

PAT: Well, you are here now, so you might as well tell me what brought you.

NICOLA: …….. it's my husband.

PAT: ………….. Your husband …………. yes?

NICOLA: There's something going on ………….. he's gotten strange ………….

PAT: Your husband is behaving strangely ……….. strangely how?

NICOLA: It's hard to explain ……….. he's not himself.

PAT: Give me an example of what you mean by strange.

NICOLA: Well …………… he looks at me funny.

PAT: He looks at you funny.

NICOLA: Yeah ………… Kind of sideways ……….. it's weird.

PAT: He looks at you funny. Hmmm. Anything else?

NICOLA: Well ……….. I feel kind of uneasy.

PAT: Has he hit you or hurt you in any way?

NICOLA: ……Noooo …… no, not really.

PAT: So he hasn't hit you or hurt you in any way?

NICOLA: Not really……. the kids are scared of him.

PAT: The kids are scared of him. What makes them scared?

NICOLA: Well, he's so angry when he comes home from work. He yells at them for the smallest thing.

PAT: He yells at them.

NICOLA: Yeah, he used to play with them, but now they hide when he comes home.

PAT: How old are they?

NICOLA: Pete is 12 and Shannon is 9.

PAT: So they spend more time in their rooms now?

NICOLA: Yeah, I can hardly keep Pete off his iPad, and Shannon plays with her dolls in her room and won't come out.

PAT: Sounds very normal pre-teen behaviour to me. Does he hit them?

NICOLA: No, he just yells, and they lock themselves in their rooms.

PAT: And what then?

NICOLA: He turns on the TV and I get him a few beers and his dinner and he drinks till he falls asleep.

PAT: Okay so we have a dad who is tired when he comes home from work who yells at the kids, then settles down to watch TV before going to bed.

NICOLA: Yeah, no one is allowed to disturb him.

PAT: What does he do if he is disturbed?

NICOLA: He yells and yells, and we all go away and leave him alone.

PAT: No violence?

NICOLA: No ……… not really ……… he's raised his fists a few times but we all know to keep out of his way.

PAT: Hmmmmmm. What is it you want me to do?

NICOLA: I dunno ………… I thought ………… maybe I should leave before something explodes?

PAT: Alright, let's work through the practical things you have to think about.

NICOLA: Okay

PAT: You can claim for a sole parent benefit, but there is a compulsory stand-down period, and it takes some time to prove that you are, indeed, a sole parent. Do you have enough money to tide you over?

NICOLA: Money? No, he does not let me have a bank account. He gives me cash for the necessary shopping and I have to give him the receipts so he can check on what I have spent.

PAT: You don't have a bank account of your own, or a credit card?

NICOLA: No.

PAT: Well, that limits things. You could always go to a women's refuge, but based on the story you told me, they would not see you as a priority case, and I know they are all over full at the moment with a waiting list. I might be able to get you a place in one out of town, but you need to understand that would involve the children changing schools.

NICOLA: That's not really a fair go for the kids.

PAT: Do you have family members you could stay with for a while?

NICOLA: No, my parents are dead, and he didn't like my sisters, so I have not spoken to them in years. I am not even sure where they live these days, and we have moved around a fair bit, so they probably don't know where I live either.

PAT: Well it seems to me your options are rather limited. We can start the process to get you a sole parent benefit but we can't really go very far with it until you are living separately from your husband and it would be better if you have started the legal process for a separation and ultimately a divorce.

NICOLA: I can't do that. He will never agree to a divorce.

PAT: If you leave him, he doesn't have to agree. You can start the process.

NICOLA: I …… I really don't think I can. He'll kill me if I leave.

PAT: Has he said so in so many words?

NICOLA: Not really….. I just know he would.

PAT: Well, if you want to change your situation, you will have to take control. Make a decision and take action. I'MAL happy to help you with an application for a benefit or to help you relocate to a refuge where I can find a space for you and the children. It's up to you.

NICOLA: It's so hard ……….. I don't know what to do.

PAT: Take your time. Think about what I have said and come back and see me when you have made a decision.

NICOLA: (stands, wringing hands) I guess so. …….. I just don't know.

PAT: (standing and ushering her to the door) Well you have some options to think about. Let me know! if you want to take action.

NICOLA leaves. Lights dim. PAT comes to sit down as before, and MAL scoots over to sit next to him/her, then lights up

MAL: So what happened next?

PAT: Someone must have seen her leaving the building and told him.

MAL: So he knew she's been talking to someone in the police building?

PAT: Yeah………… apparently he went to the pub that night and got roaring drunk.

MAL: He got drunk.

PAT: Yeah ……….. and he got a shotgun from somewhere.

MAL: A shotgun

PAT: Yeah *(puts head in hands and a long pause. Then looks up, takes a deep breath, and says)* So he went home and shot both the kids in their beds where they were sleeping.

MAL: Shot the children?

PAT: With a shotgun. They didn't have a chance.

MAL: And Nicola?

PAT: She must have tried to stop him. He beat her almost to death.

A long pause

MAL: What happened then?

PAT: The neighbours must have called the police. When they burst into the house, he was standing over her with the shotgun pointed at her.

MAL: And then?

PAT: He laughed, shot her, then put the shotgun in his mouth and pulled the trigger.

A long pause

PAT: You know, she survived. He shot off both her legs, and the scars from the beating will never fade, but she survived.

MAL: Her children didn't.

PAT: No, and she has to live with that every day of her life.

MAL: And what could you have done to prevent this?

PAT: God, I don't know .... Listened better to her?

Another long silence

PAT: There were some signs, you know, but she was just so unsure, so unclear .... but I shouldn't have let that distract me .... I should have listened more carefully.

MAL: And because you didn't, she has to live with the loss of her children and her legs for the rest of her life.

PAT: I don't know how she finds the courage to keep going.

MAL: Well YOU don't have to. You can jump, and all your guilt and pain will end.

Another long silence

PAT: Not to feel. Not to remember how I failed her.

MAL: Rather an easy way out, don't you think?

PAT: An easy way out .... I guess it is......... She doesn't have that.

MAL: No, she doesn't.

Another long silence then PAT stands up

PAT: I should not take the easy way. I should remember every day the cost of my mistake.

MAL also stands slightly behind PAT

MAL: So, in living and feeling the pain every day, you think you can atone?

PAT: I guess so. If I remember her every day, perhaps one day I can save someone, someone in a similar situation.

MAL: Perhaps so.

PAT: I know she has forgiven me. I visited her in the hospital, and she said so.

MAL: Yes, forgiven. My sister is an amazing person. But I am not so nice, and I do not forgive so easily.

MAL gives PAT a shove, and PAT falls off the bridge. MAL stands for a moment, looking down, then turns and walks away

THE END

On the Hoof

October 2021

Synopsis

Whilst we have come a very long way in addressing gender stereotypes, there are still circumstances where such stereotypes still hold sway.

Characters

- **JESSIE MELLING** – owner and operator of a large cattle station somewhere in the outback

- **RICHARD MELLING** – her husband, absent-minded professor type

- **WASHINGTON** – cook and housekeeper

- **NEVILLE PRENDERGAST** – fussy, city slicker banker, wearing a suit and tie, carrying a briefcase

The set consists of a desk/table with chair (if desk is small, could have a second side table nearby) plus 2 other chairs around the room, each with a cushion

Jessie is sitting at a desk working with some papers. Washington shoulders open the door and comes in with a tray of coffee and biscuits

WASHINGTON: Here you are, boss. You said to give you a 30-minute warning before the plane was due in. And you've been working on those papers all morning. Not even taken a break for lunch. It's not good for you, you know. Here, get this down you.

She places the tray on Jessie's desk or the side table, hands Jessie the cup, bustles about, twitching cushions on a place on the chairs, etc. Jessie looks up blearily, taking a moment to focus after her intensive concentration on the work

WASHINGTON: Ah, you with me now. Drink your coffee and have something to eat. Here…

She thrusts a biscuit into her hands. Jessie stretches and takes a dip of the coffee and a bite of the biscuit

WASHINGTON: Now, do you want the good news or the bad news?

JESSIE: (vaguely) Good news? God, I hate this paperwork. Jonathon will kill me when he sees how far behind I am. And he is coming to inspect this lot for the buyer. I just can't keep on top of it all with Sam away in the city. Why did his wife have to be so sick with this pregnancy? It's not fair!

WASHINGTON: I'm sure she thinks it's not fair either! The good news. Jonathon is not on the plane. He's got the flu and is in bed.

JESSIE: Not on the plane. Then why is it coming in then? *(She throws down a sheet of paper onto the desk)* That means I don't need to worry about these for now.

WASHINGTON: It can't be that easy. The bad news. The buyer's special banker is coming. Jonathon says he's a hopeless city slicker. Wouldn't know one end of a good lot of beef on the hoof from another.

JESSIE: Then why the hell is he coming? He can't inspect the stock I've put aside for Jonathon if he doesn't know what he's looking at.

WASHINGTON: No, indeed. But apparently, he wants to come and inspect anyway, check the genetic records, and make sure that the ones we've reserved for Jonathon's buyer are the ones we said they were before we ship them out.

JESSIE: Oh shit, then I'd better get back to these records and get them in shape.

Jessie puts the coffee and biscuit back on the tray. Washington hovers a little, then clears her throat, saying hesitantly

WASHINGTON: There is another little bit of bad news

Jessie looks up with a frown, already focused on the work and not really paying attention. She says absently:

JESSIE: What?

WASHINGTON: Well, it's Mr Richard.

JESSIE: Hmm?

WASHINGTON: You know what he's like. He's collected up a lot of bones from that last steer we slaughtered and is drying them in the oven

JESSIE: *(absently)* In the oven?

WASHINGTON: *(indignantly)* So I got the lads to put up a drying rack in the paddock out back and moved them all out there. I need me oven to cook lunch.

She waits for Jessie's reply, but she is engrossed in her work again and does not respond. She leaves. After a brief pause, Richard wanders in. He carries a notebook and pen, absently chews on the pen now and then, and occasionally opens the notebook and scribbles something in it

RICHARD: Do you know what Washington has done? Gone and destroyed my beef, that's what. Inexcusable. That beef was important.

JESSIE: *(absently)* Yes, dear *(pause then looks up briefly)* But perhaps the oven in the kitchen was not the best place for one of your experiments

RICHARD: Where else will I get good drying? Do you know what she's done? Mixed everything up, that's what. An abomination all over the back paddock. It's not on. It's just not on. How can I work like this?

JESSIE: *(looking up, speaking ironically)* How indeed. *(Goes back to her work)* I'm nearly done here. I must finish before the plane comes in. Can we talk about this later?

RICHARD: It's not on. Washington thinks she runs the place. An abomination in the back paddock. My work ruined.

He wanders out, muttering to himself. There is a pause and the sound of a plane landing. Jessie ignores it and hastens to complete the paperwork. She gives a sigh, stacks the papers tidily, and stands up just as Richard wanders back in with his notebook and pen

RICHARD: Who is that coming to disturb us? I wonder if they will help me – need to sort out the abomination in the back paddock.

WASHINGTON: Mr Neville Prendergast, boss. I must go and check me
lunch. I had to make some last-minute changes *(she glares at Richard),*
so it needs a bit of me attention. I'll bring the drinks in, in a minute.

*Washington leaves. Neville comes into the room and advances towards
Richard with his hand extended. He ignores Jessie. He is carrying a
briefcase in one hand*

NEVILLE: Ah, Mr Melling. Mr Jessie Melling? How are you? Good to
meet you. I am so interested in learning more about your beef.

RICHARD: *(absently. He passes the empty cup into the outstretched
hand)* Ah hello? Did we invite you? Who are you?

*Neville looks bemused at the cup in his hand. He doesn't understand why
he has been given an empty cup but is not sure if he should put it down
or hold on to it. He's rather offended that he is not recognised.*

NEVILLE: Ah, your beef?

RICHARD: *(It finally penetrates that Neville has mentioned his beef)*
Oh, you are interested in my beef *(he bustles around looking for his
notebook and pen, pushes Neville out of the way, finds them on the tray,
shoves his half-eaten biscuit at Neville, who has to place his briefcase at
his feet to accept the biscuit. He looks disgusted at having a half-eaten
biscuit in his hand. Richard picks up the notebook and pen and waves
the notebook angrily, making stabbing motions towards Neville with the
notebook. Neville backs off warily and trips over his briefcase)*

RICHARD: Well, that bloody Washington has taken it all. Yes, taken it
all. It's a disaster!

*Throughout this scene, Jessie remains at her desk, initially amused, then
gradually trying not to laugh. She ends up lying over the desk with her*

face in her hands. She has no inclination to rescue Nigel who has insulted her by not acknowledging her at all

NEVILLE: *(in shock, scrambles to his feet and fends off the stabbing notebook with the cup, which Richard absently takes from him. Richard then struggles to manage notebook, pen, and cup, so he puts the cup down on Neville's briefcase and sticks the pen behind his ear)* Washington has taken your breeding stock? All your beef?

RICHARD: *(warming up as someone is finally listening to his complaints)* Yes, taken the lot. I had them all safely stowed, exactly how I wanted them. Exactly, I wrote it all down here *(Richard waves up the notebook at Neville)* Now, an abomination. All over the back paddock. I shall complain. Yes, I shall complain. That Washington is a menace! It's war, I tell you. *(He stamps up and down the room, tripping over the briefcase, and kicking the cup)* I'll declare war on that Washington.

NEVILLE: Complain? A menace? *(increasingly alarmed – he looks towards Richard, scurries across the room to rescue the cup, and places it back on Jessie's desk. He looks at the half-eaten biscuit and places that down as well)* War? Surely not.

Richard continues to stomp around the room, slapping his notebook onto his hand

RICHARD: Washington. War *(under his breath, then he focuses on Neville and says clearly)*: All gone. Destroyed. Abomination.

NEVILLE: I don't understand. But they are all gone? *(anxiously. He rushes over to his briefcase and grabs it away from Richard who looked as if he was going to kick it.)*

RICHARD: Yes, all gone. What shall I do? My work is ruined

NEVILLE: This is a disaster *(he sinks into a chair, holding his briefcase tight to his chest).* I understand you have some of the best genetic lines in the world. And they are all gone. My principal will be distraught. What happened?

RICHARD: All over the back paddock. Pieces everywhere. It's an abomination.

NEVILLE: Your breeding stock is scattered all over the back paddock? In pieces? How did Washington manage that? Drop a bomb? *(He is increasingly alarmed, and his voice rises in pitch throughout whilst he still clutches his briefcase close to his chest)*

RICHARD: Drop a bomb? *(He stops pacing, looks puzzled, then his annoyance takes over)* Might just as well have done. All over the back paddock. My work is ruined *(he flings his arms in the air, and his notebook flies out of his hands, coming close to hitting Neville)*

NEVILLE: *(ducks the notebook and groans)* Ruined. My principal. He was relying on your stock to regenerate his herd. He will be distraught

RICHARD: He's distraught. I'm distraught. *(He stomps to the door to leave, then hesitates, turns and looks at Neville)* Who is your principal? Why does he care about my work? *(puzzled and much calmer)* Do I finally have someone interested in what I do? *(He goes over to Jessie and shakes her)* See, my work does matter. His principal is interested; he's distraught.

Jessie is sniggering more loudly now

JESSIE: Yes, dear

Richard leaves the room. Neville turns to Jessie

NEVILLE: Why are you laughing? This is not a joke. It's a disaster. My principal was relying on your breeding stock, and now I hear that America has destroyed it all. *(He pauses and reflects)* Why would America bomb your breeding stock? It doesn't make sense.

JESSIE: That's because it hasn't happened. The breeding stock your principal wants to purchase is right here. I have the papers for them on my desk.

NEVILLE: Papers? For cattle spread all over the back paddock? I don't think so, madam. Please call your boss back here so we can sort this out

The door opens, and Washington comes in with a tray containing drinks

WASHINGTON: Lunch will be ready in 10 minutes. Here's your drink. Help yourself. I have to go and drag Mr Richard in from the back paddock *(she leaves)*

NEVILLE: Poor Mr Melling. Contemplating the ruin of his breeding herd, is he? Here, *(to Jessie)* pour me a drink, will you? Do you have wireless – I'll call that pilot and get him to come back and pick me up. No point wasting my time.

JESSIE: No, you don't understand, Mr Prendergast. The breeding animals your principal wanted are quite safe. There is no problem. I have all their paperwork here, signed and sealed.

NEVILLE: Safe? You mean the Americans did not destroy all the herd?

JESSIE: *(giving up trying to tell the truth, and resigning herself to going with the flow)* No, indeed, Mr Prendergast. They are all safe. I can show you after lunch and you can match their numbers with those on the papers. All is fine. Come, we'd better go for lunch.

She ushers Neville towards the door, then grins wickedly, and as he leaves, she says:

JESSIE: After all, we don't want Washington to get angry with us for spoiling lunch. One of our best steers, I believe. Gathered from the back paddock. Cooked to perfection.

THE END

Rebellion

August 2024

Synopsis

An author is attempting to write a play for *Favourite Shorts* but the Characters will not co-operate. They would rather experiment with some lost opportunities from their past.

Characters

- **AUTHOR** – any age, any gender

- **EDNA** – older female

- **FRANKIE** – older female

Author is sitting at a table with paper, chewing on a pencil/pen and staring into the distance, deep in thought.

AUTHOR: (*reflectively*) I have got to get something written down to share at the follow-up writing workshop. We all promised we would do something. This is so hard. I just don't know where to start. Okay (*decisively*). We have two friends, Edna and Frankie, and they meet up in the mall and decide to go for coffee.

EDNA and FRANKIE enter and see each other.

FRANKIE: Edna. I haven't seen you for ages. How are you?

EDNA: Frankie, you're looking great.

FRANKIE: We haven't had a good chat for ages. Let's go and have a coffee.

EDNA: Good idea. Look, here's a place.

FRANKIE: Okay

They take a few steps towards the coffee shop, and then Edna stops.

FRANKIE: Are you coming?

EDNA: This is absolutely boring. Must be something better we can do.

FRANKIE: Yeah, you're right.

EDNA: Hey, you remember when we were in Buenos Aires that time and there was this bar across the road from our hotel?

FRANKIE: Yeah. It always looked busy, but we never plucked up enough courage to go across.

EDNA: It didn't really get going till quite late at night, and we weren't sure how safe we would be.

FRANKIE: I kinda regret that now, looking back.

EDNA: Well, let's go there now.

FRANKIE: Think we should?

EDNA: Why not? Let's go!

AUTHOR: No, no, no, no, no, that is not appropriate. You're going into a coffee shop in the mall.

EDNA: No, we are not! Here we are. Let's go in.

Edna and Frankie place a small table downstage.

FRANKIE: Look, here's a free table. I'll grab that. You go to the bar and get us a drink. I'll have a beer. Whatever they have on tap.

EDNA: Okay, I won't be a mo.

Edna collects 2 drinks. Frankie gets two chairs, puts them by the table, then sits. Edna comes back with two beers. She sits. They have to lean towards each other to hear.

FRANKIE: Gosh, it's loud.

EDNA: Hey, look over there - what do you think is happening?

FRANKIE: We're just in time for the floor show.

EDNA: How's that for timing?

FRANKIE: That music's got a real beat to it.

FRANKIE: Here come the performers.

EDNA: Oh my God!

FRANKIE: They're naked!

EDNA: And gorgeous!

FRANKIE: Can men be gorgeous?

EDNA: God, yes, and they're shining.

FRANKIE: That's body oil.

EDNA: Ooh la la. I've never seen anyone that big before!

FRANKIE and EDNA wave their hands in front of their faces.

AUTHOR: No, no, no, no! A gay bar in Buenos Aires is not appropriate. This is 'Favourite Shorts.' There are young performers, and there might even be kids in the audience. Not happening! We are in the mall going into a coffee shop.

Frankie and Edna remove the table and chairs.

FRANKIE: Phew, that was an experience.

EDNA: I didn't realise it was a gay bar.

FRANKIE: You know, I felt really safe there,

EDNA: Well, it's not as if we were going to be hit on, is it?

FRANKIE: Come on, Edna, we don't get hit on anywhere these days.

EDNA: Unfortunately.

AUTHOR: No gay bar, no, not going to happen. You are going into a coffee shop in the mall here in Armidale.

EDNA: Do we really have to?

FRANKIE: Where else can we go?

EDNA: Hey you remember that trip we did to New Zealand and we went to that restaurant on the top of the hill, remember, in Rotorua.

FRANKIE: Yeah, and you can go all the way down the hill in the luge.

EDNA: We looked at it, we thought about it and we went to lunch instead.

FRANKIE: Pretty boring, really, weren't we?

EDNA: How about we do it now?

FRANKIE: I'm up for it. Let's go.

Edna and Frankie grab a chair each and place them downstage. They get a steering wheel. They climb in, acting as if they are stepping over the side of a go-kart-like Luge, and sit down. Edna is driving.

EDNA: Let's go.

FRANKIE: Be careful, won't you? There's not much between us and the ground. (*pause then somewhat hysterically*) My God, we're going fast.

EDNA: Whee! Watch us go.

FRANKIE: (*shouting*) There's a corner coming up!

Edna and Frankie lean over to one side as if steering round the corner.

FRANKIE: (*shouting*) Go faster

Frankie throws her arms up in the air just like people do on a Ferris wheel. Edna looks at her and then throws her arms up too.

EDNA and FRANKIE together: Wheeeeeeee!

FRANKIE: (*panicking*) Edna, you're driving! (*Edna grabs the wheel. Pause*) There's a corner coming!

EDNA: Got it.

They both lean the other way around the corner

FRANKIE: Go faster - someone's coming up behind us.

Edna: Right, you are.

FRANKIE: Another corner!

They lean over to go round the corner, leaning further than before. They wobble and almost fall off the chairs before they straighten up.

EDNA: That was a close call.

FRANKIE: The final strait. Let's go!

Frankie throws her arms up in the air. Edna keeps her hands on the steering wheel.

EDNA: The end.

FRANKIE: That was a blast!

Edna and Frankie struggle to get out of the luge.

FRANKIE: See that little shit over there - he is the one who passed us by that last corner.

EDNA: He doesn't look any more than five or six years old!

AUTHOR: You are NOT doing the luge. You are going into a coffee shop in Armidale.

FRANKIE: Oh, what the hell. After that I think I need a coffee.

EDNA: Okay.

They remove the steering wheel, fetch a small table, arrange the chairs, and sit down

EDNA: That was fun.

FRANKIE: I'm not sure I didn't pee myself.

EDNA: (*chuckles*) It was a bit hairy in places.

FRANKIE: I think I might reward myself with a cake.

EDNA: You're living dangerously - coffee and cake.

FRANKIE: Why not? You only live once.

EDNA: We need someone to come and serve us.

They look around.

EDNA: I wish they'd hurry up. I could really do with that coffee now.

FRANKIE: I can't see anyone.

Edna looks around again, and then clicks her fingers several times and calls in a loud voice.

EDNA: Waiter, waiter!

There is no response. Both women look around again.

EDNA: (*Loudly*) Waiter, waiter?

Author looks around, sighs, puts down the pen, grabs an apron, puts it on, and goes over to the table.

AUTHOR: Sorry to keep you waiting, ladies; we are busy today.

FRANKIE: We've been here for ages.

EDNA: It's not good enough.

AUTHOR: Sorry, what can I get you?

FRANKIE: I fancy something sweet. What cakes have you got?

AUTHOR: We have chocolate, carrot, and Black Forrest.

FRANKIE: I don't fancy any of those. I'd rather like a piece of cheesecake.

AUTHOR: I don't think we have any cheesecake left.

FRANKIE: Well, it's what I fancy. Check for me?

AUTHOR: Won't be a moment (*goes out the back, pauses, returns*)

AUTHOR: I'm sorry the cheesecake is all gone.

EDNA: While Frankie is trying to figure out what she wants from your pathetic menu, I want a lactose-free hot chocolate.

FRANKIE: Oh, that sounds nice. I'll have one of those - make it nice and frothy.

EDNA: What else have you got?

AUTHOR: Vanilla slice, chocolate doughnut and more in here.

Edna swivels around and looks behind her. Author walks upstage a little towards an imaginary counter and points.

EDNA: Can't see.

AUTHOR: Caramel slice, peppermint crunch, apple turnover.

FRANKIE: I'll have the caramel slice.

AUTHOR: You ordered a lactose-free hot chocolate. Are you aware that the caramel slice has lactose?

FRANKIE: I don't care. It's what I fancy.

AUTHOR: As long as you are aware.

EDNA: Now me. I'll have the carrot cake.

AUTHOR: The carrot cake has cream cheese icing. It is not lactose-free.

EDNA: I know what I want.

AUTHOR: Very well. We'll have two lactose-free frothy hot chocolates, a caramel slice, and a piece of carrot cake.

FRANKIE: And be quick. We've been waiting long enough.

Author exits. Frankie and Edna drum their fingers on the table waiting. In a short while, Author reappears with two mugs and sets them down on the table

FRANKIE: This isn't frothy enough.

AUTHOR: I'm sorry, it's the best we can do with lactose-free milk.

EDNA: It's not good enough. We ordered it frothy. That means we want it frothy.

FRANKIE: Where are our cakes?

AUTHOR: They will be here in a minute.

EDNA: This place really sucks.

FRANKIE: The service is shit, and they can't even do a frothy hot chocolate.

AUTHOR: (*slams the order pad down on the table*) You know what? I'm done! I'm sick of you two.

AUTHOR (*stalks over to the writing table, grabs the pad, and tears off the page where s/he had been writing*) I'm done, finished, had enough. (*storms off stage down the corridor to the foyer*)

Edna and Frankie high-five.

EDNA: Got him/her *pause*

FRANKIE: Hey, if s/he is not going to write about us, does that mean we don't exist?

They look at each other in horror.

EDNA: Oh shit, what have we done?

They stand up in a hurry.

FRANKIE: (*loudly*) Come back. Come back. We didn't mean it!

EDNA: (*loudly*) We'll be good, promise!

They run out following Author, and you can hear their voices fading into the distance as they run down the corridor.

EDNA and FRANKIE: Come back. Come back. We'll be good.

THE END

The ways of a snowflake

July 2024: Read at Armchair Theatre August 2024 and amended September 2024

Synopsis

In modern society, there is an increasing focus on respecting the rights of others; of behaving in ways that are inclusive and support people with different skills and expectations to participate. This play questions how that is enacted when what is needed to enable someone to participate fringes on breaching the rights of others. How far do we go to enable everyone to participate? Do we have the right to expect others to change their behaviours in significant ways in order to make us feel comfortable?

Characters

- **EVANGELINE THOMAS**

- **MARY SOLAS** - a counsellor

- **PERSON 1**: male (plays JAMIE, MAURICE, MALCOLM, PERSON A)

- **PERSON 2**: older female (plays MRS SOTHERBY, BEATRICE [Evangeline's mother], JANELLE, PATRICIA, FIONA, PERSON B)

- **PERSON 3**: female (plays CLARICE, BETSY, MICHELLE, PERSON C, SUSAN)

NB: The Characters played by PERSONS 1, 2, and 3 are all small roles, but they can all be played by separate actors if preferred. However, at a minimum, three actors are required to cover these roles.

Scene 1: Mary's office, and a Gym

The scene is set in Mary's office – Mary is a counsellor. Mary is sitting behind a desk. There is a small coffee table and 2 chairs in front, or to the side, of the desk. The coffee table holds a few magazines and a box of tissues. There is a small wastepaper basket beside the coffee table.

There's a knock on the door. Mary stands up, walks around the front of her desk, and calls, "Come in."

Evangeline enters

MARY: Lovely to see you again, Evangeline. Have a seat!

Evangeline smiles a little uncomfortably and sits down in an armchair. Mary sits down in an armchair opposite her.

Evangeline: Hey. *(She twists the strap of her handbag in her hands.)*

MARY: Let's just quickly recap where we are before we begin. Last week, you explained how lonely you feel, and you wondered if there was something in the way you interacted with other people that seemed to drive them away and make it really difficult for you to maintain any long-term relationships.

Evangeline nods

MARY: Okay. We talked about some things that happened in your past. I'd really like to go back to something you described to me. Remember you talked about an incident at the gym when you were a young teenager?

EVANGELINE: *(nods)* I remember.

MARY: How about you tell me a little more about that?

EVANGELINE: *(begins hesitantly but gains confidence)* I guess I must have been about 13 or 14. We had just got a new gym built in town. It was the only one in town, and they put in, I think, four trampolines. I'd never seen a trampoline before. None of us kids had and we were all super keen to have a go. They offered lessons, and lots of kids in town signed up - thinking back, I suspect many more than they had planned for. Anyway, I used to go along on a Thursday after school. There were about 20 kids in my group, and that meant we spent a lot of time lining up and waiting for a turn. They would only let one kid at a time on each trampoline.

MARY: That makes sense.

EVANGELINE: Yeah, I guess so. It was a safety issue. I just remember being so frustrated that I spent most of my lesson time waiting for a turn.

MARY: So, the waiting felt like forever.

EVANGELINE: Sure did. There was this one kid in my class. His name was Joshua, I remember that. I've never liked that name. I guess these days, he would have been labelled ADHD, but back then, he was just this naughty kid who ran around all over the place and caused trouble and wouldn't wait quietly in line.

MARY: He caused challenges for all of you.

EVANGELINE: Yeah, he used to push in front of people instead of waiting his turn, and I remember feeling really cross when it seemed his bad behaviour resulted in him having more turns on the trampoline than me. It wasn't fair.

MARY: That must have been really frustrating. Last week, you mentioned one particular incident.

EVANGELINE: Yeah, it was probably halfway through the term. This particular day Joshua was really annoying, and I think the coach was getting really pissed off with him as well because he kept pushing in front of everybody when he wasn't running around the gym yelling at the top of his voice.

MARY: So, tell me what happened.

EVANGELINE: It was my turn next, and I was really excited. I wanted to try the flip our teacher had demonstrated. I felt like I had been waiting forever. Anyway, just as the kid ahead of me was getting off the trampoline and I was getting ready for my turn, Joshua pushed me away and jumped on in my place. I tripped and fell down, and I was so angry.

MARY: And?

EVANGELINE: The teacher told him to get off, that it wasn't his turn, but he refused. I felt more and more angry because we had a timer so that we all got the same amount of time each turn, and he was wasting my time, and the timer was ticking down. I think the teacher was really cross as well because he stepped onto the trampoline and tried to grab him. As Joshua was bouncing, he came down quite hard and banged into the teacher, and they both fell over. Joshua started screaming and said he hurt his ankle. The teacher pulled him off the trampoline and made him sit down on the floor. He was still screaming. The teacher told me to get on for my turn, but I'd only had time for a few bounces before the timer went off, and the next kid in line wanted his turn. It wasn't fair.

MARY: And what happened next?

EVANGELINE: I think the teacher gave him an ice pack to put on his ankle. I didn't get another turn on the trampoline that day because our class finished. It wasn't fair. I was putting on my shoes when his grandmother came to collect him.

Lights go down from the counselling office and come up in a gym. Jamie, the trampoline teacher, is talking to Mrs. Sotherby, Joshua's grandmother. The aim is for this interaction to become increasingly heated as it progresses.

JAMIE: Joshua has a twisted ankle. I've had it iced but it mightn't be a bad idea to have it checked out just in case.

MRS. SOTHERBY: How can this have happened? You are supposed to be looking after my grandson.

JAMIE: It was an accident. Joshua pushed in front of other children and jumped on the trampoline when it wasn't his turn. I asked him to get off but he refused, so I joined him on the tramp to help him off but he bounced into me and we both fell over.

MRS. SOTHERBY: This is not good enough. I have a good mind to report you. Your rules say only one person on the trampoline and you have broken your rules. Why couldn't he have been left alone to finish his turn?

JAMIE: It wasn't his turn, Mrs. Sotherby. He had pushed in front of the children, who had all been waiting for their turn.

MRS. SOTHERBY: That doesn't matter. You broke the rules.

JAMIE: So did Joshua, Mrs. Sotherby. He did not wait his turn. He pushed in front of others. That is not acceptable.

MRS SOTHERBY: I pay for him to bounce on the trampoline, not to stand in line and waste his time waiting.

JAMIE: Well, as you can see, Mrs. Sotherby, with four trampolines and 20 children enrolled in the class, it is not possible for any child to monopolise a trampoline. They all have to take their turns. We have a timer with a bell to make sure that every child gets the same amount of time. Everyone is treated fairly.

MRS. SOTHERBY: That is not good enough. You shouldn't have accepted that many enrolments in the class. I pay for Joshua to bounce on the trampoline, not to stand in line.

JAMIE: All the children have the same amount of time on the trampoline. We have kept a limit of 20 children so that no child is waiting for too long to have a turn and each child gets multiple turns every lesson.

MRS. SOTHERBY: I don't care about these other children. I pay for my Joshua to bounce on the trampoline, and I expect him to be able to do so for the entire duration of the lesson.

JAMIE: I'm sorry that is not possible.

MRS. SOTHERBY: Well, you need to make it possible.

JAMIE: I'm sorry, I cannot do that.

MRS SOTHERBY: Then I shall complain to the owner. I know him – we play golf together. This is absolutely not good enough. Not only are you incompetent in managing enrolments, you clearly have no idea how to follow the rules. I will get you sacked.

JAMIE: You are, of course, welcome to lodge a complaint about the classes if you wish to do so. If you go to the front office, the receptionist will give you the details of the complaint process. If you will please excuse me, I need to talk to some of the other parents.

MRS. SOTHERBY: Don't walk away from me. I am talking to you.

JAMIE: Good afternoon, Mrs. Sotherby.

Jamie turns away. Mrs. Sotherby reaches out, grabs him by the shoulder, and spins him around.

JAMIE: Please do not touch me, Mrs. Sotherby. There are other parents here with whom I need to speak. Excuse me.

As Jamie turns away, Mrs. Sotherby swings her handbag and hits Jamie in the arm.

Lights dim and come back up in the counselling room

MARY: So that was quite a volatile exchange.

EVANGELINE: Yes, I remember sitting there waiting for mum to come and get me and trying at the same time to hide behind the shoe rack.

MARY: Did you think Mrs. Sotherby was going to hit you?

EVANGELINE: Looking back, common sense says no, but the loud voices and the anger frightened me, and I wanted to disappear. It was scary that suddenly a place that had been fun and safe now felt really dangerous. It wasn't fair to me to have to see that.

MARY: So, what did you do then?

EVANGELINE: Mum came to get me, and I was glad to get out of there. She was really cross when I told her what had happened.

MARY: How did you feel when you went to trampoline class the next week?

EVANGELINE: I worried about it all week, and by the following Thursday, I felt quite sick. I told mum I didn't want to go.

MARY: You didn't go back?

EVANGELINE: No. Mum said I didn't have to complete the term if I didn't want to, so I never went back.

MARY: And were you happy with that decision?

EVANGELINE: Sometimes, when the kids at school talked about what they were doing in trampoline class, I thought it might be fun to go back, but whenever I thought about it seriously, I started to feel sick.

MARY: Did you ever go to the gym again?

EVANGELINE: *(reflectively)* You know I don't think I've set foot in a gym ever since. I know years later some of my friends were using the gym for aerobic classes and that sounded fun but I could never bring myself to join them.

MARY: There are other gyms in town now.

EVANGELINE: Yes, I know, but I just don't fancy going to a gym. It's not my thing.

Lights down.

EVANGELINE: (reflectively – can be done in half-light as if dreaming, or a voice-over in the dark)

Bouncing.

Flying.

Tingles of fear.

Will I land in the right place?

Perhaps not so high.

More control is the thing.

I want my turn.

It's not fair.

Loud voices.

It's not fair.

I fell over.

It's not fair.

Noise and anger.

It's not fair.

Shouting.

It's not fair.

I want out of here.

It's not fair.

It's not fair.

Scene 2: Mary's office

Mary's office as before. Mary is fussing around, plumping the cushions and fiddling with the magazines on the coffee table. There is a knock at the door.

MARY: Come.

The door opens, and Evangeline enters.

MARY: Good to see you again, Evangeline. Have a seat.

Evangeline sits and fiddles with the strap of her handbag. She doesn't look directly at Mary. Mary also sits and pauses for a minute, but Evangeline says nothing.

MARY: We talked last week about an incident at the gym when you were a child, but today, I'd like to spend some time looking at the incident you mentioned that happened at the pub. I think it was when you were working in your first job, wasn't it?

EVANGELINE: (*hesitantly*) Yes, I was working in this office, and people liked to go to the local pub on Friday after work.

MARY: Can you tell me some more about that?

EVANGELINE: Well, I was still really new at the job, and I thought it would be a good way to get to know the people I worked with a little better.

Mary waits, but Evangeline says no more.

MARY: That sounds like a really sensible thing to do.

EVANGELINE: *(still hesitant)* I guess. I'd been there about a month before they invited me to come. I'd never felt particularly comfortable in a pub, but I thought I should make the effort.

Another pause before Mary prompts.

MARY: Yes, indeed.

EVANGELINE: So, I went along this one Friday night and I felt really uncomfortable. People were drinking and laughing and there was lots of loud talk and I didn't know who to talk to and I couldn't hear anyone anyway.

MARY: *(after a pause)* Yes?

EVANGELINE: Umm, I sat nursing a drink – it was a soft drink, actually – for ages, and I wondered how soon I could leave without being rude.

MARY: *(after a pause)* Yes?

EVANGELINE: And then this man came and sat down beside me and started talking to me. He had to put his face really close to mine for me to hear him. I felt really yucky. I'd heard some of the others in the office talk about him. Apparently, he tried to date all the office girls at some point, and his breath smelled of the beer he had been drinking.

MARY: So, you felt really uncomfortable.

EVANGELINE: I felt trapped. I wanted to leave, but I didn't know how to.

MARY: What did you do?

EVANGELINE: I couldn't really hear what he was saying so I just kept nodding and smiling and when I felt sick to my stomach, I pushed my chair back and stood up and muttered something about going to the bathroom.

MARY: And then what?

EVANGELINE: The bathroom was on the other side of the room, and I had to walk past the bar to get there. I kept looking over my shoulder to make sure he wasn't following me.

MARY: (*after a pause*) Was he?

EVANGELINE: No.

MARY: (after a pause) Go on.

EVANGELINE: (hesitantly) There were a number of men leaning on the bar drinking, and as I got close to them, I heard that two of them were having an argument.

MARY: (*after a pause*) They were shouting at each other?

EVANGELINE: They were really loud, and one was swearing and saying horrible things to the other. It was awful. I put my head down and tried to hurry past.

MARY: (*after a pause*) And then?

EVANGELINE: I think one of them must have pushed the other because he stumbled back and crashed into me. The next thing I knew, I was on the floor covered in beer, and he was lying on top of me.

MARY: That must have been a real shock.

EVANGELINE: I felt trapped. I felt suffocated. I tried to get up, but he was heavy, and he wasn't moving, and I couldn't breathe. It was awful. The doctor said afterwards that I had had a panic attack. I thought I was going to die. I couldn't breathe, and my heart felt like it was jumping out of my throat. I couldn't do anything. (*She is really distressed now, grabs a tissue from the box on the coffee table, wipes her eyes, and blows her nose. Mary indicates the rubbish bin beside the table for the tissue.*)

MARY: (*waits until she calms*) So, what happened next?

EVANGELINE: (*she grabs another tissue and uses it to dab her eyes occasionally*) Someone must have pulled him off me but I don't remember anything until later when I was sitting in what, I think, was the manager's office at the pub and the doctor was with me.

MARY: A really, really frightening experience for you.

EVANGELINE: (*vehemently*) I never went out for work drinks again. Just thinking about it makes me feel sick, and I can't breathe.

MARY: Do you think that impacted your relationships with colleagues at work?

EVANGELINE: Some of the girls laughed at me. They told others at work. It was quite a joke apparently. I didn't want to know them any better. If they thought it was funny, I didn't want to know them. It wasn't right.

MARY: Did they tell you that?

EVANGELINE: I heard them gossiping in the staffroom. Behind my back. I had to work with them but I certainly did not have to socialise with them.

MARY: Was there anyone at that job that you liked and met outside of work?

EVANGELINE: No! (*quite angrily*) I am not interested in people who get their kicks out of getting drunk and making lots of noise.

MARY: So, at that point in your life, you were not socialising with any of the people with whom you worked. What did you do for social interaction?

EVANGELINE: I liked going to museums and art galleries, and I would often sit in the park near my house and read.

MARY: Did you do these things alone?

EVANGELINE: Oh yes, I like the peace and quiet.

Lights down.

MARY: (reflectively – can be done in half-light as if dreaming, or a voice-over in the dark)

Fear is understandable.

Nerves.

Anxiety.

But limiting.

So limiting.

You have to want to engage.

You have to want other people.

But fear limits.

Fear prohibits.

Fear tells you loneliness is okay.

Fear says stay safe.

Don't reach out.

Stay safe.

Stay safe.

Alone is safe.

How do I reach her?

How do I help her unlearn?

Can I do this?

Am I good enough for her?

Scene 3: Café

The setting is a small cafe. Beatrice is sitting at a table for two with an open wine bottle and two glasses of wine. She is busy texting on her phone. She looks up and frowns and then goes back to texting on her phone. Evangeline rushes in looks around, sees her mother and hurry across to the table and sits down.

EVANGELINE: Sorry I'm late. The traffic was awful.

BEATRICE: You need to plan ahead, dear.

EVANGELINE: Have you ordered?

BEATRICE: Yes, dear. (*She puts her phone down on the table and looks at her daughter critically*) I ordered you a salad. I think that was a wise choice. Have you put on a little weight?

EVANGELINE: I don't think so.

BEATRICE: Then perhaps it's that outfit you're wearing, dear, it doesn't really suit you.

EVANGELINE: It's comfortable.

BEATRICE: (*sarcastically*) It looks comfortable.

There is a short silence.

BEATRICE: How are you, dear?

EVANGELINE: I'm fine, thanks, mum, and how are you?

BEATRICE: Oh, busy as usual. I have the annual charity ball coming up, and, predictably, most of the organisation has been left to me.

EVANGELINE: Because you're so good at it, mum.

BEATRICE: That's true. You wouldn't believe the fuss over the theme this year. Can you imagine that common Mrs. Johnson wanted to have a showgirl theme? I mean, really, how tacky.

EVANGELINE: I imagine Mrs. Johnson would look amazing in a showgirl costume. She has the figure.

BEATRICE: That may be true, but she certainly does not have the style.

EVANGELINE: I'm trying to imagine you in a showgirl costume.

BEATRICE: (*snaps*) Not funny, Evangeline.

EVANGELINE: Sorry, mum.

BEATRICE: (*still cross*) Do you have to call me by that common diminutive?

EVANGELINE: Sorry, mother.

There is another long pause. Beatrice's phone dings, she picks it up and responds to a text message then puts it down again.

BEATRICE: Tell me about work, dear. How is it going?

EVANGELINE: It's all a bit stressful, actually. My office is lovely, but it seems that everybody wants to congregate in the corridor to chat, and if I leave my door open, the noise drives me nuts. I can't concentrate.

BEATRICE: You just have to tell them that their noise is disturbing you and ask them to chat somewhere else. Really, Evangeline? Stand up for yourself.

EVANGELINE: It's not really that simple. The water cooler is in the corridor close to my office and people seem to want to chat when they refill their water bottles.

BEATRICE: Don't be a weakling, Evangeline. If they are annoying you, you have a perfect right to ask them to be quiet and to have their chats elsewhere.

EVANGELINE: It really seems as if the water cooler is social central.

BEATRICE: How inconsiderate of your needs.

EVANGELINE: Yes, it is frustrating, but otherwise, the work is really enjoyable, and I think I am doing very well there.

BEATRICE: What are the chances of promotion?

EVANGELINE: It's a big company with a number of offices throughout the country. They do have a staff intranet and often advertise vacant positions via that before they go external.

BEATRICE: Think very carefully before you apply for a transfer somewhere else. You need to be sure that you can find a safe place to live with the right kind of amenities close by.

EVANGELINE: Yes, I know, mother.

BEATRICE: I'm not sure that you do.

EVANGELINE: I will think very carefully, mother, before making any changes.

BEATRICE: And, of course, consult with me. I have a lot more experience in these matters than you.

EVANGELINE: Yes, mother,

BEATRICE: What about the romantic front? Are you seeing anybody?

EVANGELINE: Not really.

BEATRICE: You need to be thinking about it, Evangeline. You're not getting any younger.

EVANGELINE: Yes, I know, mother.

BEATRICE: Nobody looking at me would think that I am old enough to be a grandmother, but I really do think it is time you gave me grandchildren, Evangeline.

EVANGELINE: Yes, mother.

BEATRICE: Are you making sure you go to the right kind of places where you can meet the right kind of men? Safe places.

EVANGELINE: Yes, mother. I spend time each weekend at the museum and art gallery.

BEATRICE: But do you make an effort to speak to anyone?

EVANGELINE: It's not that easy, mother.

BEATRICE: You need to be more determined, my dear.

EVANGELINE: Yes, mother.

BEATRICE: I do hope you are trying.

EVANGELINE: Yes, mother.

BEATRICE: And I do hope you have given up that silly volunteer role on the front counter at the art gallery. Serving behind a counter is demeaning.

EVANGELINE: Yes, mother.

BEATRICE: Here comes the waiter with our food at last. Now, make sure you eat all the salad, Evangeline; it is good for you.

EVANGELINE: Yes, mother.

Lights down.

BEATRICE: (reflectively – can be done in half-light as if dreaming, or a voice-over in the dark)

They fly away and leave you,

When you have done so much for them.

Nights staying home to supervise.

No one else to share the load,

No escape from the responsibility.

You have given up so much for them.

So much.

And do they appreciate that?

Do they even think about what you have done for them?

What you have sacrificed?

What you have given up.

And they make so many mistakes.

So many mistakes.

And you want to help them,

But they don't listen.

They don't listen.

Don't repeat my mistakes.

Learn from me.

Don't make my mistakes.

Make a better life for yourself.

You should have a better life.

Trust what I try to teach you.

Trust I know the mistakes to avoid.

But they don't listen.

Why can't I put my head on her shoulders?

Make the right decisions.

Don't make my mistakes.

Don't make my choices.

Live a better life.

Be happier.

Be safer.

Not my mistakes.

Please.

Trust me.

I know.

Learn from me.

I know.

Scene 4: Mary's office, and a meeting room

Mary's office. Evangeline and Mary are sitting in their usual places

MARY: You were telling me last week about a book club that you had joined. Tell me more about that.

EVANGELINE: I love reading and so talking about books with other people who love reading seemed sensible and safe. When I saw a book club advertised at the local library, I thought it would be a perfect thing to do to meet people.

MARY: Indeed, it does. Tell me some more.

EVANGELINE: Well, the first week was a little difficult because I hadn't had a chance to read the book they were talking about, so I sat there and listened to the conversation and tried to figure out who I might like to get to know.

MARY: Tell me about the people there.

EVANGELINE: The thing is run by this woman named Janelle and that first meeting there were about eight people there including me so it's not a huge group. I didn't get everyone's name that first week, and it turned out that not everybody came every week, so there was often someone new at each meeting.

MARY: Were there some regulars who were there most of the time?

EVANGELINE: Yeah, there was a guy named Bernard and another, I think, called Sean, and a woman called Clarice. I rather liked Clarice the first few times there, and so after a few weeks, I made a point of sitting next to her and talking to her. I thought we had quite a bit in common and after one of the meetings, we even went out for a coffee.

MARY: That sounds really positive.

EVANGELINE: Yes, I thought things were going quite well, and I even told mother that I had found a new friend.

MARY: She would have been pleased about that.

EVANGELINE: Yes and no. She wanted to know a lot more about her, but I didn't know how to answer her questions because I didn't know that much about Clarice. She told me not to jump into a friendship too quickly until I knew more about her.

MARY: What do you think she was worried about?

EVANGELINE: I really don't know. I have never figured out what mum is thinking. (*pause*) I guess the bottom line is she wanted to be sure that I was safe.

MARY: Why did she think you might not be safe being friends with Clarice?

EVANGELINE: I have no idea.

MARY: Tell me more about your friendship with Clarice.

EVANGELINE: We didn't get very far. We still only met at the book club and we went out for coffee afterwards a few times. Not every week.

MARY: And?

EVANGELINE: Then we were assigned *Black and Blue* by Veronica Gorrie to read. Do you know it? It's a story of an Aboriginal woman who worked as a police officer and fought for justice both within and beyond the Australian police force. It won the 2022 Victorian Premier's Prize For Literature and the 2022 Victorian Premier's Literary Award For Indigenous Writing. I thought it was awful. I hated it. I thought about not going to the discussion because I thought it was just so unnecessarily violent and ghastly. I didn't want to even think about it, but I had arranged to meet Clarice for a coffee after the discussion, so in the end, I went.

MARY: And what happened?

EVANGELINE: Some people in the group said they thought it was a really good book talking about topics that needed to be shared, but others hated it. The issues of racism and sexism really got people going. *(pause, then continue thoughtfully)* It seemed to me that if people didn't break the law, then they wouldn't get punished, and I wasn't the only one thinking that. One of the guys, Maurice, I think, said something to that effect.

Blackout. Lights come up with a group of people sitting in a semi-circle.

MAURICE: I think too much fuss is made about disadvantages. It seems to me it's an excuse for laziness. If people would only get their butts into gear, they could succeed.

JANELLE: You've got to be kidding me. Do you have any idea what it's like to have to work twice as hard as any man in order to get any recognition?

MAURICE: Rubbish. We have lots of women in high powered jobs. Those who don't make it are just not good enough, or just don't work hard enough.

CLARICE: That's just not true. There is lots of evidence that women don't get promotions and still don't get equal pay.

MAURICE: If women worked as hard as men and were committed, then they would get the promotions.

JANELLE: What world are you living in? There is clear evidence that women are still discriminated against in the workplace. Just look at the gender pay gap.

MAURICE: Sure, there are more women in lower-paying jobs, but what do you expect when you take years off work to look after the kids? When you do come back to work, you're not there half the time because the kids need you for this, that, and the other. If you want the promotions and the high-paying jobs, you've got to put in the hours.

CLARICE: And what does that say about the culture of the workplace that you are only a valuable employee if you work more than the hours for which you are paid?

MAURICE: You have to show commitment to the job.

JANELLE: Are you saying commitment to the job is only demonstrated by working extra hours?

CLARICE: If you are any good at the job, you shouldn't need to work extra hours.

MAURICE: And anyway, the book is about women in the police force. How can they do the job properly?

CLARICE: What do you mean?

MAURICE: Police work surely requires strength - how is a woman going to break up a fight between two strong drunks or face down an angry gang member?

JANELLE: Policewomen have been doing that for decades,, and anyway, who says fighting is the best way to manage a conflict?

MAURICE: Oh, so you reckon the lovey-dovey talk fest is the way to go.

CLARICE: There's no need to be rude. De-escalating conflict is better than going in boots and all.

MAURICE: Nah. We need more good old-fashioned policing – give them a show of strength. You need to show who is boss.

CLARICE: So, you are saying that strength and masculinity are more important than open and frank discussion.

MAURICE: A show of strength beats namby-pamby talking every time.

EVANGELINE: (*timidly*) Are we getting off the subject of the book?

MAURICE: There's a typical female intervention for you. You can't defend the argument that strength is important so now you want to change the topic of the discussion.

Evangeline huddles back in her chair and looks down. She doesn't engage anymore in the conversation.

CLARICE: That's not fair, Maurice. We are here to discuss the book.

MAURICE: We are discussing the book. We are saying that it's all very well to use gender and race as an excuse, but the bottom line is if you can't do the job properly, get out.

JANELLE: That's not at all what the book is saying. I think there are clear examples of how gender and racism impacted the author and made it a million times more difficult for her to do the job.

MAURICE: So, we're back to where we started. Making excuses is not good enough. You either do the job properly, or you get out. Don't make excuses.

CLARICE: (*angrily*) Maurice, you're being very unfair. That is not what the book is saying. The sexism and racism faced by the author are horrendous, and quite honestly, I don't think things have changed very much.

MAURICE: Another female making excuses for her own weaknesses.

CLARICE: (*Her voice volume is escalating with anger.*) Maurice, you *are* deliberately obtuse. Let's look at some of the examples in the book and tell me how the author could have behaved differently.

MAURICE: Not interested, darling. I thought the whole thing was rubbish from beginning to end. Just an excuse for inadequacy.

CLARICE: (*very angry*) How dare you! How dare you criticise someone who has worked so hard and made a difference in this world?

MAURICE: Oh, so the little female is trying to justify this waste of space of a book.

CLARICE: Maurice, you're an arsehole.

JANELLE: keep it down, you two – we are here to discuss the book, not get personal.

Lights dim and come back up in Mary's office

EVANGELINE: Clarice was so very angry. I felt really unsafe. We didn't go out for coffee that night. And as the week went on, I felt more and more nervous about going back to the book club.

MARY: What were you thinking?

EVANGELINE: I went to the book club for civilised conversation. What had happened was absolutely not civilised, and I felt unsafe.

MARY: You described a loud-voiced argument. Was there any physical violence?

EVANGELINE: No, nothing like that.

MARY: So, it was the argument in loud voices that upset you.

EVANGELINE: I felt unsafe.

MARY: Did you tell them how you were feeling?

EVANGELINE: No, I just wanted to get out of there.

MARY: Perhaps it might be useful in our next session if we practice how you might tell people when you feel uncomfortable.

EVANGELINE: (*doubtfully*) If you think it will help.

MARY: Let's practice some of the things you could say when you are feeling uncomfortable.

Lights down.

EVANGELINE: (reflectively – can be done in half-light as if dreaming, or a voice-over in the dark)

Loud voices.

Shouting.

Anger.

Violence.

Uncontrolled.

Fear.

Trembling.

Heart pounding.

Can't breathe.

Get me out of here.

Get me out of here.

Don't shout.

Sounds in my head.

Jangling around.

Spiking in my skull.

Pain.

Fear.

Get out of here.

Go away.

Leave me alone.

Leave me alone.

Leave me alone.

I am not safe.

Not safe.

Scene 5: Café

Evangeline is sitting in a cafe in the art gallery with a coffee next to her. Nearby is another table with two women, Betsy and Patricia, who also have coffees. They are talking loudly enough for Evangeline to overhear their conversation. Whilst their conversation is loud and animated, they do not get angry – they are 2 friends who are comfortable with each other and able to argue without causing offence.

BETSY: I don't know how you cope with that bloody mutt. You know he pulled my coat off the peg at the back door and chewed a bloody great hole in the pocket.

PATRICIA: I guess he was trying to get the treats in the pocket.

BETSY: He should know better.

PATRICIA: He's a dog.

BETSY: I had a real struggle to patch up my coat.

PATRICIA: It's a dog walking coat. It doesn't matter what it looks like.

BETSY: I know that, but that's not the point.

PATRICIA: Well, what is the point?

BETSY: I shouldn't have to hide my clothes away whenever your mutt comes around.

PATRICIA: He's not a mutt. He's a pedigree designer dog.

BETSY: With the manners of a mutt.

PATRICIA: He's only a puppy.

BETSY: And he's going to continue to behave like a puppy unless you crack down on him. He needs to learn how to behave.

PATRICIA: He behaves perfectly well for me at home. Maybe there's something you're doing at your place that makes him naughty.

BETSY: So now you're saying it's my fault your mutt is badly behaved.

PATRICIA: Well, he's not badly behaved at home.

BETSY: I don't want any more of my clothes ruined, so you can keep your mutt at your place.

PATRICIA: Where I go, my baby goes.

BETSY: You're going bananas, woman. He's a bloody dog, not a baby.

Evangeline has been showing increasing discomfort as the argument progresses and at this point, she stands up and crosses tentatively over to the table.

EVANGELINE: (*timidly*) Excuse me. Your loud voices are making me feel unsafe. Could you please leave?

BETSY: Who the bloody hell do you think you are to ask us to leave? You shouldn't be listening to our conversation, and if you don't like it, you can leave.

EVANGELINE: I have a right to enjoy my coffee in peace, and you are disturbing me.

BETSY: Then don't listen to our conversation.

EVANGELINE: I don't feel safe with you at this table next to me.

BETSY: Then bloody move.

PATRICIA: Let's just keep this civilised. We will talk more quietly. Will you please go back to your table?

BETSY: Don't pander to the bloody snowflake. If she doesn't like sitting at a table near us, then she can move.

Evangeline looks scared and backs away from the table. She gathers up her belongings and hurries away. As she leaves, she mutters to herself:

EVANGELINE: Disgraceful behaviour in a public place. I shouldn't have to put up with it.

Lights down and come up in Mary's office.

EVANGELINE: Telling them how I felt was a complete waste of time and I felt even more unsafe.

MARY: Let's review what you said.

EVANGELINE: I told them their loud voices made it impossible for me to enjoy my coffee in peace, and I asked them to leave.

MARY: Is their leaving the only possible solution to the problem?

EVANGELINE: What do you mean?

MARY: Let's look at the problem.

EVANGELINE: I don't understand.

MARY: What do you think was the main problem?

EVANGELINE: They were arguing where I could hear them.

MARY: And is the only solution to this problem for them to leave?

EVANGELINE: Either that, or they stopped arguing and talked quietly.

MARY: Is there nothing else?

EVANGELINE: Well, I don't see why I should have had to move. I have a right to enjoy my coffee in peace. The only decent thing for them to do would have been to leave.

MARY: I want you to think of something you could have done to make you feel more comfortable.

EVANGELINE: What could I have done? I don't know. Leave, I suppose.

MARY: You said their loud conversation made you uncomfortable. Is there anywhere else you could have sat in the café where you might not have heard them?

EVANGELINE: But why should I move? I was there first.

MARY: True. But could you have done something to make you feel more comfortable?

EVANGELINE: I did something. I left.

MARY: You did, indeed. Can you think of another way you could have handled this situation? Another way to help you feel more comfortable? Perhaps something where you could still enjoy your coffee without their conversation making you feel uncomfortable.

EVANGELINE: Are you saying that I should change where I was sitting?

MARY: I'm not telling you what to do Evangeline. I'm simply suggesting there are different ways to handle the situation and I want you to think of different strategies YOU could use to make you feel comfortable rather than expecting other people to change what they are doing.

Lights down.

Mary and Evangeline both speak reflectively – can be done in half-light as if dreaming, or a voice over in the dark but they are unaware of each other – they are each in their own worlds.

MARY: Defining the problem.

EVANGELINE: I have a right to feel safe in a public space.

MARY: Defining the problem means identifying what the real issues are.

EVANGELINE: They were speaking loudly and sounded angry.

MARY: Defining the problem effectively opens up options for solutions.

EVANGELINE: We should behave responsibly in public spaces.

MARY: Why did she feel unsafe? We know that.

EVANGELINE: I hate loud voices.

MARY: Loud voices signal anger.

EVANGELINE: People need to control themselves.

MARY: Anger triggers fear.

EVANGELINE: Control means safety.

MARY: Perhaps control means feeling comfortable, and feeling comfortable means feeling safe.

EVANGELINE: I have a right to feel safe.

MARY: Are others responsible for our safety, or are we ourselves?

EVANGELINE: If I don't feel safe because of something you are doing then you need to stop doing it.

MARY: Do others have to change to allow me to feel safe, or do I have to change something in my situation? Who is responsible for my safety?

EVANGELINE: You should not behave in ways that make me feel unsafe.

MARY: Who is responsible for my feelings of safety?

EVANGELINE: When you shout in public, I feel unsafe. You need to learn how to behave.

MARY: But why didn't she simply move to where she couldn't hear them? Why is her safety someone else's responsibility? Am I my brother's keeper? Who is responsible for my safety? Is it you, or is it me?

EVANGELINE: I have a right to feel safe.

Scene 6: The Park and Mary's office

Evangeline is sitting on a park bench reading a book. Malcolm walks across and pauses at the bench.

MALCOLM: Excuse me, do you mind if I sit here?

EVANGELINE: *(looks up from her book and smiles slightly)* That's fine.

Evangeline continues to read. Malcolm sits down, and it is quiet for a minute.

MALCOLM: Hello, I'm Malcolm. I've seen you several times here at the park.

EVANGELINE: Yes, I really enjoy being here. It's such a lovely space. I'm Evangeline.

MALCOLM: That's a lovely name. Pleased to meet you, Evangeline.

EVANGELINE: Do you live nearby?

MALCOLM: I have an apartment on the other side of the park, and I walk through here every day to go to work.

EVANGELINE: Oh really, where do you work?

MALCOLM: I'm an accountant - I work in that large office block on the other side of the park – the one on Waverley Street.

EVANGELINE: That's funny. I work in the solicitors' office in that same building. We are on the 10th floor.

MALCOLM: I'm on the sixth. How funny is that?

EVANGELINE: I walk through the park to go to work, too, though I must admit when the weather is bad, I sometimes take the bus and go all the way around the park to get to work.

MALCOLM: It can be pretty miserable walking through here in the rain and in the winter coming home when it gets dark early.

EVANGELINE: I always take the bus in the winter when I'm going home in the dark. I love this park, but I don't feel safe walking alone in the dark.

MALCOLM: Very sensible. I must admit there have been a couple of times when I've felt a bit uneasy coming through here in the dark. Do you know there's a legend that puts a bushranger in this park?

EVANGELINE: You are kidding me.

MALCOLM: No. This area used to be a forest, and 200 years ago, there was a tavern over on the corner of Waverly Street and Blenheim Road and a small village over by the lake.

EVANGELINE: But what would bring a bushranger here? The villagers can hardly have had anything worth stealing.

MALCOLM: No, indeed. The legend has it that the bushranger was the son of the pub owner and used to keep his horses in his father's stables at the pub. The story goes that he was betrayed by his lover, who worked as a barmaid at the pub, after she found him consorting with a lady customer.

EVANGELINE: What happened then?

MALCOLM: The soldiers came to the pub to arrest him, and he ran out into what was then the forest in his nightwear. They chased him down and captured him, and he was hung from one of the trees nearby.

EVANGELINE: (*with a shudder*) A gruesome end. And now you're going to tell me that his ghost wanders this park.

MALCOLM: No, not HIS ghost. The story goes that the barmaid regretted her actions and threw herself from the roof of the pub.

EVANGELINE: So, they were reunited in death - a romantic story.

MALCOLM: Perhaps so.

EVANGELINE: And how is it that you know the story?

MALCOLM: I'm a member of the local historical society, and the story was written in a private journal from that time. It was amongst a pile of papers donated to our group recently. I have been spending some time each weekend sorting through all the papers and cataloguing them.

EVANGELINE: That sounds really interesting.

MALCOLM: Yes, I enjoy playing with history. You know we are always looking for volunteers to help us with our work. We get a lot of donations, and everything has to be looked through very carefully and catalogued.

EVANGELINE: Maybe someday I'll come along and see what I can do to help.

MALCOLM: You would be very welcome. I am there every Saturday morning but if you want to come at another time then just ask for Louise. She is the manager and I can let her know that you might pop in sometime.

EVANGELINE: That would be great.

There is an awkward silence for a moment, and then Malcolm stands

MALCOLM: Well, I'd better go and leave you in peace to finish your reading. It was lovely to meet you, Evangeline, and I hope we catch up again sometime.

EVANGELINE: Maybe I'll see you walking to work one morning.

MALCOLM: Bye for now.

EVANGELINE: Goodbye Malcolm.

Malcolm walks off. Evangeline watches until he has gone and then returns to reading her book. Lights down, then come up in Mary's office

EVANGELINE: He seemed a nice man. I thought about going to the museum that Saturday but I didn't want to look as if I was chasing him. Then I thought about going last Saturday, but I got nervous and didn't go to the museum – I stopped in the park and stayed there instead. I was a little cross with myself because I hadn't bought my book with me, so I felt a little silly sitting in the park without it. I kept telling myself to go to the museum, but I couldn't find enough courage.

MARY: Do you think you might find the courage this Saturday?

EVANGELINE: I'd like to.

MARY: What do you think might stop you?

EVANGELINE: I don't know. (*There's a long pause.*) People can be so unpredictable. You never know what will make them angry, and then I feel unsafe.

MARY: What would make you feel comfortable working as a volunteer in the museum?

EVANGELINE: (*after a pause*) I guess knowing that I can leave any time.

MARY: And if you went into the museum, could you leave at any time you wanted to?

EVANGELINE: Yeah, I guess so.

MARY: So, given you know you can leave any time, do you think you can find the courage to try it?

EVANGELINE: I guess so. Why not?

Lights down.

MALCOLM: (*reflectively – can be done in half-light as if dreaming, or a voice-over in the dark*)

Is this the beginning of a new chapter?

Will you join me in exploring this new thread woven into our lives?

Strangers connecting.

Finding commonalities.

Exploring new lands.

Together?

Perhaps.

Do you want to walk with me?

Shall we gaze on this world together?

What will we see that is new?

What will we build?

Will our togetherness be better than the sum of our parts?

Will we begin?

I'd like to try.

Would you?

I wonder.

Will you?

Will you walk with me?

Share my world.

Can we build together?

Lives shared.

Friendship, love.

Delightful possibilities.

Together.

Exciting.

Potential.

Scene 7: Café

Evangeline and Malcolm are sitting in a cafe with a coffee each.

MALCOLM: I really enjoyed that new exhibition.

EVANGELINE: I think it was something of a new direction for the art gallery to take -exhibiting costumes - but I found it fascinating.

MALCOLM: The work involved in some of those pieces was incredible.

EVANGELINE: It must have taken them hours and hours especially when you consider that they were made before we had sewing machines, so all done by hand.

MALCOLM: I was imagining how difficult it would be to get dressed in some of those outfits.

EVANGELINE: I guess they would have had servants to help them.

MALCOLM: They would have needed to.

EVANGELINE: I really loved the embroidery on some of those dresses. It was incredible. It's kind of inspired me. I did a bit of embroidery as a kid and I wonder if I could make myself a blouse. Something like the ones we saw - probably not as fancy, though.

MALCOLM: If you're clever enough to do that, perhaps you should think of joining the local drama society. I'm sure they would appreciate a hand with costume making.

EVANGELINE: I suppose so.

MALCOLM: My mum was really active in that group for a long time and they were always on the lookout for people who could help them.

EVANGELINE: Is she still involved?

MALCOLM: No, she gave it up a few years ago. She says she finds it so hard to see to thread the machine and she can't do any of the fine hand sewing any more.

EVANGELINE: That must be frustrating for her.

MALCOLM: I guess so. She says it's the price she pays for getting old.

EVANGELINE: A price we will have to pay at some point.

MALCOLM: For sure, but not for a good many years yet.

EVANGELINE: I hope not.

MALCOLM: What are your plans for the weekend?

EVANGELINE: I'm not really sure.

MALCOLM: There is a footy game at the local stadium on Friday night, and I'd like to go. Would you come with me?

EVANGELINE: I don't cope very well with large crowds.

MALCOLM: I have seats in the members' stadium. That area tends to be quieter than the public areas.

EVANGELINE: No, thank you. I don't like crowds. They make me feel unsafe.

MALCOLM: The members' stand has security, and you can't get in without showing your membership status. It's quite safe.

EVANGELINE: No, thank you. I don't want to go anywhere where there are crowds. Lots of people make me feel unsafe. How about we go to that nice restaurant? The one just down the road from the art gallery is nice.

MALCOLM: Could we do that on Saturday night? I really would like to go to the footy on Friday.

EVANGELINE: Saturday night doesn't suit me.

MALCOLM: Oh, rats. I'd really like to see you this weekend. Is it really only Friday night that's possible?

EVANGELINE: Yes.

Malcolm: Well, maybe I can give my tickets to a friend. How about I check that out with him and let you know tomorrow?

EVANGELINE: Okay

Lights down briefly and then come up – the following are a series of short scenarios that could be done in front of the curtain

MALCOLM: The autumn parade is on this weekend. Let's pop downtown and have a coffee and watch it.

EVANGELINE: I'd rather not go to the autumn parade. There are too many people, and I don't feel safe.

Pause

MALCOLM: I'd really like to see the new movie that came out this week.

EVANGELINE: I'm told there's lots of violence in it. I don't like violence.

MALCOLM: I'd like to see it. I might go with one of my friends tomorrow night.

EVANGELINE: But don't you want to do things together with me?

Pause

MALCOLM: My friends are going fishing for the long weekend.

EVANGELINE: Oh really. What shall we do that weekend?

MALCOLM: I'd like to go with my friends. I haven't been fishing for ages, and I haven't spent much time with them lately.

EVANGELINE: You're thinking of going away for the whole weekend without me?

Pause

EVANGELINE: I'd really like to go to that travelling exhibition at the art gallery.

MALCOLM: Yes, it looks interesting. How about Sunday afternoon?

EVANGELINE: There are probably lots of people out and about on Sunday afternoon. I think it will be really popular. I'd rather go straight after work on Thursday night. There are often not many people there then.

MALCOLM: It is nicer to look at the paintings when there are not lots of people jostling for space, I agree. But I have a work thing on this Thursday evening. Bill is leaving and I've worked with him for years.

EVANGELINE: It's only on for a few days, so if we don't go Thursday we'll probably miss it, and I'd really like to see it. We won't get another chance.

Pause

MALCOLM: (*speaking firmly but not loudly*) We need to talk. It seems that we always have to do what you want and never anything I want.

EVANGELINE: But you want to do things where I don't feel safe. I have a right to feel safe.

MALCOLM: Absolutely, but I have a right to do the things that make me feel happy some of the time.

EVANGELINE: Please don't yell at me. I don't like it.

MALCOLM: I am not yelling. I am speaking clearly and firmly.

EVANGELINE: It sounds like yelling to me. I don't like it.

MALCOLM: It seems to me that everything has to be your way or the highway.

EVANGELINE: If you yell at me, I will walk away. I can't do this.

MALCOLM: I am not yelling at you. I am telling you how I feel.

EVANGELINE: I can't do this.

She exits

MALCOLM: *(to himself)* Your way or the highway, it's looking like it might be the highway.

He exits and lights down.

EVANGELINE: (*reflectively – can be done in half-light as if dreaming, or a voice-over in the dark*)

Why does he push?

Push.

Push.

Push.

I want to do this. I want to do that.

What about me?

It isn't fair.

I want to share.

I do.

Why is it his way or my way?

Why can't we find OUR way?

Together.

Aren't we better together?

Stronger united.

Two people as one.

Or are we two people on overlapping tracks.

Touching occasionally.

But not forever.

My silent rooms are filled with haunting fears.

Am I safe with him?

People are so unpredictable.

Do I really know him?

Am I safe?

Scene 8: Kitchen/break room of Historical Society

Fiona and Michelle are sitting in the kitchen of the historical society having a coffee each.

FIONA: This new exhibition has been a lot of work, but I think it's looking good now.

MICHELLE: Yeah, there are only a couple of finishing touches we have to do.

FIONA:, Where is Evangeline?

MICHELLE: I think she's just finishing up that last piece she was researching.

FIONA: She's done a really good job.

MICHELLE: Yes, when Malcolm introduced us, I was a little uncertain of her but she's really come through and done a great job.

FIONA: (*pause*) You've got the rosters all organised for the opening weekend?

MICHELLE: Yes. You are on Saturday morning and me Saturday afternoon with Breanna, Josie and Patrice all doing a couple of hours each. Evangeline has volunteered to do all day Sunday. Malcolm will come in Sunday afternoon and Morgan will double up with Evangeline Sunday morning.

FIONA: That's great. It's always difficult to get people on Sunday so Evangeline is a lifesaver - willing to do all day.

MICHELLE: We're all organised for this weekend's opening. I'll wait and see the level of interest in the new display before I work out rosters for the next few weekends.

FIONA: That makes sense. Sometimes, having just one person is plenty.

MICHELLE: I am hoping this new display will generate some interest.

FIONA: We could certainly do with a few more volunteers to help out.

MICHELLE: I think we can always do with some new volunteers. It's not enough just to maintain what we have.

FIONA: Creating new displays is such a lot of work.

MICHELLE: I enjoy the research that goes into them.

FIONA: That's more your thing. I enjoy playing with the aesthetics - making the display look attractive.

Evangeline enters.

MICHELLE: Grab a cuppa and join us. You've been working really hard, Evangeline.

EVANGELINE: Yes. I finally tracked down some more information about that clay pipe you were worried about.

MICHELLE: Really?

EVANGELINE: I was looking through that old diary – you know, the Josephine Barton one. I found a reference to a pipe that her father used, and I think it just might be the one we have.

FIONA: What makes you think that?

EVANGELINE: In the diary, Josephine talks about her father regularly smoking a clay pipe

FIONA: Yes, he had several of them by all accounts. He preferred the longer stemmed ones and they broke so easily.

MICHELLE: Some accounts said they sometimes broke after only one use.

EVANGELINE: Josephine made a comment about a clay pipe in her diary. Her father bought one home from one of his trips overseas that was a little more special. It had some carving around the bowl.

MICHELLE: The one we have has carving around the bowl. I wonder how common that was?

FIONA: We know the maker's mark was often stamped into them.

EVANGELINE: The records say that clay pipes became less common after 1850 when briar was used more often but according to Josephine's diary, her father preferred to use clay pipes and continued to do so for quite a good many years.

FIONA: There are records of clay pipe moulds being used in this area for quite a long time after that – at least up until World War I.

MICHELLE: We've always assumed that the clay pipe we have was one of these much later versions because it doesn't have a date stamp. We believe that is characteristic of the pipes made in the early part of the 20th century in this area.

EVANGELINE: I read up about those. I'm wondering if this particular pipe came from a lot that was imported from Holland. Pipes from Holland were typically polished and this one looks like it's been shiny in the past.

FIONA: And?

EVANGELINE: Josephine writes about a shiny pipe her father bought home that had carvings around the bowl. I think the one we have might be the one she was writing about.

MICHELLE: Can you write up a little card about that (*pause*) but make it clear it's not proven? It's just something we think.

EVANGELINE: Sure. I'll do that before I go home.

MICHELLE: And you're okay for being on the roster to work all day Sunday? It's a lot to ask a volunteer.

EVANGELINE: No, it's fine. I have nothing special to do and I'm happy to be here. I think the new exhibit works really well and I'll love to show people around and talk to them about it.

MICHELLE: We really appreciate your time.

Evangeline smiles and sips her coffee. There's a slight pause.

FIONA: I'm keen to follow up with you about that old manuscript we were talking about yesterday.

MICHELLE: I know you think it's important, but I haven't had time to look at it.

FIONA: I really do think it's important.

MICHELLE: (*impatiently*) Yes, you've told me that several times. I said I will look at it as soon as I get a moment. It's been really busy this week getting organised for the opening of the new display.

FIONA: As I said to you, I think the manuscript could be incorporated into the new exhibit.

MICHELLE: There's no evidence that it links in, in any way at all.

FIONA: If you read it, you will see that there might well be connections that we can explain.

MICHELLE: Yes, you've said so, but it's not a priority. It can wait until I have time.

FIONA: I really think you need to make the time. It could be important.

MICHELLE: (*sarcastically*) Oh as important as that fake comb you pestered me about last month?

FIONA: I know that was a mistake. I've already said I'm sorry, but I don't think I have made a mistake this time.

MICHELLE: Well, your record is certainly not sterling in that area. Is it?

FIONA: Come off your high horse. We all make mistakes. None of us are perfect.

MICHELLE: But your mistakes caused me a lot of stress and wasted time and I don't have any more time to deal with another one.

FIONA: That's not fair.

MICHELLE: Life isn't fair. Suck it up.

FIONA: Now you're just getting nasty.

MICHELLE: I'm sick of you pestering me about this. Just leave it alone.

FIONA: And I'm sick of you not trusting me

MICHELLE: It's not as if I don't have precedent.

FIONA: Are you going to hold that mistake over me for the rest of my life?

MICHELLE: Quite possibly, especially if you don't shut up about this manuscript.

As this argument gets increasingly heated, Evangeline looks more and more nervous and at this point quietly put her cup on the bench and leaves the room. Michelle and Fiona don't notice she has gone.

FIONA: You're just being a bloody cow. (*She puts her cup on the bench and walks out*).

Michelle calmly finishes her coffee, puts her cup on the bench, and exits.

The next scene is performed in semi dark/complete dark with the two Characters speaking reflectively and unaware of each other's presence.

EVANGELINE: I am so disappointed. I expected more civilised behaviour from them.

MICHELLE: She left. She walked out, leaving a message to say our behaviour was impacting her mental health.

EVANGELINE: I hate it when people can't behave properly.

MICHELLE: Her mental health. Really!

EVANGELINE: I didn't sleep well that night. I kept hearing their angry voices.

MICHELLE: She left us completely in the lurch. Such selfish behaviour.

EVANGELINE: Those angry voices go round and round in my head, and I can't stop them.

MICHELLE: I had terrible trouble trying to organise someone to cover for this Sunday when she was supposed to work.

EVANGELINE: Round and round and round.

MICHELLE: And then Malcolm decided he wouldn't come in on Sunday either.

EVANGELINE: I have to look after myself.

MICHELLE: I ended up having to cover a lot of that time which made my life incredibly difficult. One of these days my partner is going to reach a limit and demand I spend more time at home with the family.

EVANGELINE: I have to look after my own well-being.

MICHELLE: So bloody selfish of her. It's not as if she had anything to do with the argument between me and Fiona.

EVANGELINE: I have to look after my own well-being.

MICHELLE: She could have just pulled up her big girl knickers and got on with it. It was none of her business.

EVANGELINE: I have a right to feel safe.

MICHELLE: Even if she wanted to come back, I'm not sure I would want to have her. Clearly, I cannot trust her.

EVANGELINE: They need to behave appropriately so I feel safe working with them. Clearly that's not going to happen.

MICHELLE: People are just so precious these days.

EVANGELINE: I have a right to feel safe.

MICHELLE:

Bloody snowflake.

I just need people to do what they say they will do.

Nothing fancy.

Nothing too challenging.

Just be reliable.

Just do what they commit to.

I don't have time to run around and pander to them.

I can't baby everyone who comes through this door.

I don't ask any more than they volunteer to do.

I don't demand more of them than they are happy to give.

So why do I spend more time stroking their egos

Than I spend doing the research I want and need to do.

Why are people so fragile.

For goodness sake, suck it up and get on with it.

Bloody snowflake.

Evangeline: I have a right to feel safe.

I have to look after myself.

I am important and I have to care for myself.

Scene 9: Mary's office

Mary's office. Evangeline and Malcolm and Mary are sitting around the coffee table. Throughout the scene, Malcolm keeps his voice level and calm despite how frustrated or angry he is feeling, though his feelings need to be evident in his body language.

MARY: Malcolm asked to come along today because there were some things he wanted to talk with you about Evangeline, and he thought it might be helpful if we had the discussion here.

EVANGELINE: *(to Malcolm)* I don't know what you think we need to come here for when we can talk at home.

MALCOLM: There are some things I want to talk about, Evangeline, and I think you will feel safer in this environment.

EVANGELINE: That sounds ominous.

MALCOLM: I hope not. I have tried to talk with you about some of these things.

EVANGELINE: Very well, fire ahead.

MALCOLM: When we decided to move in together, I agreed to move into your apartment because I understood it was familiar to you and you felt safe there.

EVANGELINE: Yes, you agreed to that.

MALCOLM: I did, but I want to make the point that from the very start of our relationship, I have always considered your feelings.

EVANGELINE: I never said you hadn't.

MALCOLM: But there have been quite a few occasions lately where you have acted as though I never consider your feelings.

EVANGELINE: That's nonsense.

MARY: Perhaps it might help, Malcolm, if you were able to share some specific examples.

MALCOLM: Alright. *(He pauses in thought)* I am a member of the local footy club and I always buy a season ticket so I can go to everyone of their home games.

EVANGELINE: And?

MALCOLM: Since I have been with you, I have not gone to a single game.

EVANGELINE: That's been your choice.

MALCOLM: You could say that, but the reality is whenever I suggest going to a game, you make it impossible.

EVANGELINE: I have told you before. I don't like crowds. I don't feel safe there.

MALCOLM: And I accept that. I have suggested numerous times that I go to a game and if you prefer, you can stay home, but you make a fuss about that.

EVANGELINE: What do you mean?

MALCOLM: You make me feel like I'm being totally unreasonable to want to go to a game without you.

EVANGELINE: But aren't we meant to do things together?

MALCOLM: We can and we do things together, but there are times when there are things I would like to do, and I don't insist that you do them with me if you don't want to.

EVANGELINE: But you want to do things that I don't like. Things where I feel unsafe.

MALCOLM: I understand that, and I don't insist that you do them. I leave the choice up to you, but I should not be stopped from doing some of the things I like just because you don't like them.

EVANGELINE: Well, if it upsets you so much, go to your silly games.

MALCOLM: I think you're missing the point here.

EVANGELINE: So, what is the point?

MALCOLM: The point is that you consistently expect me to do what you want, and you don't ever consider what I want.

EVANGELINE: That's not fair.

MARY: Perhaps it would help if you were to give another example, Malcolm.

MALCOLM: Okay, let's talk about the other night.

EVANGELINE: What other night?

MALCOLM: I was watching the footy on TV and you were finishing up some work on the computer. You came in just as the second half started do you remember?

EVANGELINE: Oh yes. I was ready to relax and watch some TV.

MALCOLM: Yes, and I said I would like to watch the remainder of the game.

EVANGELINE: But I don't like football.

MALCOLM: I understand that, and I didn't ask you to watch with me for that very reason.

EVANGELINE: But we don't have another TV, and I wanted to watch TV.

MALCOLM: And you couldn't wait until the end of the game?

EVANGELINE: But I wanted to watch TV to relax.

MALCOLM: My point exactly. You wanted to watch TV and you were not prepared to wait so I could finish watching the game.

EVANGELINE: But it's my TV.

MALCOLM: Yes, and I live in your apartment because you asked me to move in. I did suggest we both relinquish our apartments and together get something new for us but you didn't want that.

EVANGELINE: But I feel safe in my apartment.

MALCOLM: I understand that, but you still act as if it's your apartment and there are times you make me feel an unwelcome guest. It is not our apartment. It is your apartment.

EVANGELINE: I don't want to find another apartment.

MALCOLM: I understand that, but wherever we live, as long as we are together, it needs to be our space, not just your space.

EVANGELINE: Anyway, when you watch your football, you end up shouting. You yell at the ref, and you yell at the players. I HATE that.

MALCOLM: When have I ever raised my voice with you?

EVANGELINE: Just because you have not yet, does not mean you will not.

MALCOLM: I try really hard around you not to raise my voice. You even get mad at me when I'm just showing enthusiasm. I have to talk in this flat, boring voice that is just not me.

EVANGELINE: What do you mean?

MALCOLM: Just the other day, I was telling you about this big win I had at work, and all you could do was bitch at me for raising my voice at you.

EVANGELINE: It sounded as if you were shouting.

MALCOLM: I wasn't shouting. I was just talking, perhaps a little louder than usual, because I was happy and excited. You sure killed that moment.

EVANGELINE: I don't understand what you want.

MALCOLM: (*with increasing frustration and struggling to keep his emotions out of his voice*) I want to be considered an equal partner in this relationship.

EVANGELINE: You are an equal partner.

MALCOLM: No, I am not. Everything we do is done the way you want and when you want. What I want is never considered.

EVANGELINE: That's not fair.

MARY: Malcolm has given two examples where he has given you what you want without any consideration of what he wants. Can you give us an example, Evangeline, of where you have compromised to enable Malcolm to have something that he wants?

EVANGELINE: He wanted us to move in together.

MARY: And from what I understand, moving in together meant Malcolm giving up his apartment and joining you in yours. Did he suggest that you both relinquish your apartments and get a new one together? One that belonged to you both equally?

EVANGELINE: Well, yes, but it seemed silly when I like my apartment and I'm comfortable there and it's big enough for us both.

MARY: So, another example of Malcolm giving you what you want.

EVANGELINE: *(getting upset)* This is silly. I don't like this conversation.

MALCOLM: I suspect that is because you can't think of any situation where you have compromised to allow me to have something I want.

EVANGELINE: *(more upset)* You are both not being fair.

MALCOLM: I think I am being very fair Evangeline. I am asking to have this conversation with you because I want our relationship to work, but right now, it is not working for me.

EVANGELINE: What do you want from me?

MALCOLM: I want to be treated like an equal partner in this relationship. I want you to show that you think about me when you are making decisions.

EVANGELINE: I do think about you.

MALCOLM: But your decisions are always about what you want and what is best for you.

EVANGELINE: I need to feel safe.

MALCOLM: I understand that when you feel in control you feel safe, but a relationship is about two people. If you can't trust me to share in making choices in ways that I know will allow you to feel safe then I wonder about our future.

MARY: Perhaps it could help if you could tell Evangeline what you think your relationship could look like if it was working for you.

MALCOLM: I want an equal partner. I want someone who is willing to make some compromises for me. I want someone who shows that what I think and want are important to her.

EVANGELINE: But the things you want make me feel unsafe.

MALCOLM: It seems to me that you use safety as an excuse, Evangeline. How could you finding something to do for half an hour while I finished watching my game on TV make you feel unsafe?

EVANGELINE: But you know I don't like football.

MALCOLM: And I wasn't asking you to watch it. I simply asked you to let me finish watching the game.

EVANGELINE: But it's my apartment.

MALCOLM: There we have it. It seems you are not willing to make any compromises to make our relationship work. It's your way or the highway.

EVANGELINE: I don't like this conversation. I don't feel safe here anymore.

Evangeline jumps up and rushes out of the room, very upset.

MALCOLM: I have tried. God knows how hard I have tried, but I just can't keep doing this anymore. It's always about what she wants, never about me. I can't even be enthusiastic about anything if I show it in my voice. I certainly can't raise my voice. Ever.

MARY: What do you think you will do now?

MALCOLM: Trying to talk to her here was my last-ditch approach. I'm done. It's time for me to move on before I am so crushed under the weight of her requirements that I lose any sense of who I am. I just can't be me when I am around her.

Lights down.

MALCOLM: *(reflectively – can be done in half-light as if dreaming, or a voice-over in the dark)*

Did I leave some action undone?

Could I have done something different?

Was there a pivotal point I missed?

Is there something I could have said?

Some word that would have put us on a different path?

Something that would have bound us together,

And not pulled us apart?

Some word that would free her from her past?

Unravel the chains.

Open her to possibilities.

Or was I just not the right person to reach her.

Not her knight in shining armour.

Just the court jester.

Dancing around her without connecting.

Old memories, old actions, old thoughts.

An impenetrable miasma.

Ineffectual I.

On the outside.

Always on the outside.

I feel so alone in my head.

Glorious togetherness was a dream.

Unattainable.

I tried.

I tried so hard.

But I tried alone.

In the end I can only be what I am.

Changing.

Mutable.

But ultimately what I am.

And I was not enough.

Scene 10: Evangeline's apartment

Evangeline is in her apartment speaking her diary into her phone

EVANGELINE: Dear diary. I can't believe how many insensitive jerks there are in the world today, and I seem to attract more than my fair share of them. How could Malcolm say those things he did? He was totally unreasonable. How could I ever have thought I loved him when he is so insensitive and didn't care about my feelings at all. What a jerk. And how dare Mary have him in one of my counselling sessions and ambush me like that. I know she asked if he could come but she should have warned me what to expect. I will never trust her again, and I certainly won't be going back for any more counselling sessions. She betrayed me.

You know, diary, sometimes I think it would be better to just focus on my cats and forget about other human beings. They always let me down, and just when I think we might have something going, they show their true colours. Nobody cares about my feelings. Nobody gives a shit about what I want and what I feel. People suck.

There's that song in Avenue Q when one of the puppets sings: "The world is a big scary place," and you know Diary, I have to agree. People seem to get worse and worse every year. I don't remember when I was a kid, people were as nasty to each other as they are now. And kids are supposed to be antisocial beasts. What is it that makes people so selfish and so uncaring about others? I don't remember ever feeling so unsafe before. It seems these days, everywhere I go, people are yelling at each other. There's violence everywhere, and I feel so unsafe just putting my head out the front door. You know, I'm not even sure I would feel safe sitting and reading my book in the park anymore. That's where I met Malcolm, and look how badly that turned out. He seemed so nice, but underneath it, he certainly wasn't. How can I trust my judgement anymore?

I'm so unhappy at work as well. I can stay in my office and try to ignore the people around me but their nastiness can't be escaped. The noise, the arguments, the yelling, the demands all just keep piling in. When I don't hear their voices, I get their emails, and they are just as bad. The disrespect is appalling. It seems good manners are lost, and all I get are rude demands: do this, do that. I hate the rudeness; it makes me feel so unsafe. There is no respect shown to me at all.

Lights down then come up and we have a sequence building into a frenzy. As the frenzy builds Evangeline curls into a tighter and tighter ball and hides her head.

PERSON A: Hurry up and bring me that file. I need it now.

PERSON B: Move over.

PERSON C: You're in the way. Move.

PERSON A: Get me a coffee.

PERSON B: You're late with that report? Where is it?

PERSON C: The damn photocopier is jammed - who left that paper in there? Some slack bastard!

PERSON A: Shit, it's raining.

PERSON B: For God's sake, would somebody unpack the bloody dishwasher?

PERSON C: Who left that mess in the staffroom?

PERSON A: That damned case is driving me nuts.

PERSON B: Waiter, for fuck's sake, hurry up.

PERSON C: Return the bloody book to the shelf.

PERSON A: Stop mucking about.

PERSON B: It doesn't work like that.

PERSON C: Bloody hell, what do you think you are doing?

PERSONS A, B & C together: Evangeline, where the hell are you? I need you. Fix this bloody report. Now.

Lights down, then come up on Evangeline in her apartment again, speaking into her phone

EVANGELINE: Dear Diary. Another day, but perhaps not another dollar. I just couldn't stand the work environment anymore. The sheer disrespect. The anger and violence. I felt so unsafe I actually vomited all over my boss the very last time he yelled at me. I left. I can't go there anymore. I will look for work that I can do at home. Surely, these days after COVID, there must be some job that I can do 100% from home. I don't want to go out of my apartment again.

Lights down.

MARY: (*reflectively – can be done in half-light as if dreaming, or a voice-over in the dark*)

There are battles I have not won,

Fights with no victor.

Lives unchanged,

Challenges not conquered.

What good am I,

 If I can't triumph?

Or at least make some impact.

Positive, of course.

I ask myself.

Did I do right?

Could I have done differently?

Was I enough?

And myself answers.

Did it do right?

I did my best.

Could I have done differently?

I don't know.

Was I enough?

Could anyone have been enough?

Is that a cop-out.

Am I making excuses?

My reflection shows someone who tried.

But for her it was not enough.

A project left unfinished.

Chances missed.

Steps not taken.

Too little, too late.

The shadow of failure.

But I will rise.

I will rise.

Can she?

Scene 11: Street outside Evangeline's apartment

The scene is on the street outside Evangeline's apartment. Malcolm and Susan enter, strolling hand in hand.

SUSAN: Didn't you used to live over there?

MALCOLM: Oh God, yes, I did. It was the worst time of my life.

SUSAN: That bad?

MALCOLM: I felt like everything I am was being slowly crushed out of me. It took me a good year after I left to begin to feel like myself again.

SUSAN: Did you really love her that much?

MALCOLM: I thought I did at the time but looking back I honestly don't know. Can you love someone who doesn't give you any space to be yourself? I was constantly treading on eggshells around her, scared to say anything that might upset her. Given the tiniest things upset her it was an almost impossible task. I felt like I was constantly failing.

SUSAN: Doesn't love mean respecting the person your partner really is?

MALCOLM: Well, that surely wasn't my experience, and having gone through that, I'm convinced that accepting a person for who they are is a crucial component of love.

SUSAN: We are getting philosophical. I hope you know that I love you for exactly who you are.

MALCOLM: You don't know how much that means to me.

They hug each other and exit slowly, walking hand in hand.

Lights dim and come back up to spotlight Evangeline standing by herself in the middle of a bare stage.

Lights down.

EVANGELINE: *(reflectively – can be done in half-light as if dreaming, or a voice-over in the dark)*

The world is broken.

Stop, I want to get off.

Please let me get off.

Please.

I stand at my window.

At night in the silence.

The moon shines lonely,

But soft and gentle.

Leaves rustle.

But shadows move in the darkness.

Shadows and danger.

I sometimes hear the birds dawn calling.

So happy and hopeful.

The world is clean and fresh.

And I wonder,

Could I go there?

Could I be part of the gentle quiet?

But there are always others.

Contaminating the peace.

Bustling through their lives,

Destroying the serenity.

The cats meow.

Their needs are basic.

Food, water, a litter box and cuddles.

I can do that for them.

No. Stay inside.

It's safe here.

Calm, predictable, tranquil.

I will stay safe.

I am enough, for me.

My world is pulled tight around me.

A cocoon

Wrapped snugly.

I am enough, for me.

I keep myself safe.

I trust me.

I am safe.

But alone.

THE END

Strongman

May 2024: Read at Armchair Theatre June 2024 and amended July 2024

Synopsis

There is considerable interest at present in the phenomenon of the strongman, a trend that poses significant challenges to democracy[1]. Strongmen are authoritarian and build a personality cult around themselves, supported in the main by those who feel disenfranchised, outcast, and marginalised. Hughes[2] argues that strongmen aim "to destroy the positives of modernity – science and reason, tolerance of dissent, human rights and equality, and accountable democratic government – and exacerbate modernity's core pathologies – violence; materialism and greed; and inequalities based on a hypermasculinity which denigrates love and care." This play traces the development of a strongman and the growing gap between political rhetoric and the reality of the everyday lives of one family. The play is set in Australia in the early 2020s.

Characters

- **HARRIET BAXTER** – grandmother, in her 70-80s

- **REBECCA ROXON-** mother, in her 50s

- **JAKE ROXON-** father, 50-60s

- **JESS ROXON-** adult daughter, 20-30s

- **NELSON WILSON** – Jess' boyfriend, 20-40s

- **PETER SAMUELSON** – politician – Trump-like. Can be pre-recorded and projected or can be performed live. Throughout the

---

[1] Gabriel, Y., The allure of strongman leaders, in *The Routledge Critical Companion to Leadership Studies*, D. Knights, H. Liu, and O. Smolović-Jones, Editors. 2024, Routledge: New York. p. 1 - 14.
Allen, M., The Logic of Populism and the Politics of the Strongman, in *Encyclopedia of New Populism and Responses in the 21st Century*, J. Chacko Chennattuserry, M. Deshpande, and P. Hong, Editors. 2023, Springer Nature Singapore: Singapore. p. 1-4.
[2] Hughes, I., Vladimir Putin and the Pathologies of Modernity, in *Psychoanalytic reflections on Vladimir Putin. The cost of malignant leadership.* 2024, Routledge: London. p. 1 - 9. page 1.

play, he gives a number of one-liners that also can either be projected or done live – unless identified otherwise, the cast is unaware of him as he is not actually present with them.

Scene 1

Jake is sitting, lounging on a chair, and playing on his phone. Harriet is knitting and watching something on her iPad. The setting is the lounge room of the family home, an average middle-class Australian home. The door slams off stage, and Rebecca comes in wearing a jacket and conservative office clothes. She is clearly in a bad mood.

REBECCA: Hi mum (*then looking at Jake*) Hey.

Jake grunts and doesn't reply

HARRIET: Hello, love. Good day?

REBECCA: Absolutely shit. (*Speaks to Jake*) I see you've not dug the garden yet.

Jake grunts and doesn't look up from his game

Rebecca stomps out of the room and we hear another door slam off-stage

HARRIET: She's not happy, is she? Again. That new teaching job is really getting to her.

JAKE: (*looks up*) I'll make us all a cuppa.

He leaves the room. Harriet continues to knit. Rebecca comes back minus her jacket and wearing slippers instead of shoes. She throws herself into a chair next to Harriet.

HARRIET: Jake's gone to make a cuppa love. Sit down and relax.

Harriet reaches and turns off her iPad but continues to knit

REBECCA: Has he done anything today or has he sat there all day playing his games?

HARRIET: Give him a bit of space love. It's not easy losing your job at his age and there's not much he can do about it. No one will employ him at his age.

REBECCA: Yeah, I know but it all sucks! It's not fair he lost his job. It's not fair we couldn't pay the mortgage on my wage and end up having to come and live with you.

HARRIET: Love if you hadn't come to live with me, I would've had to sell the house. Prices have gone up so much, but my pension has not. I couldn't afford to keep living here.

REBECCA: You never said anything.

HARRIET: I didn't want to worry you. I could not manage looking after this house - the expenses were just too much and my pension just would not stretch any further. And there's so much I couldn't do myself anymore.

REBECCA: Yeah, well, we agreed to do a lot of the stuff around here for you, but from what I can see, he's been sitting around wasting time instead of getting on with things. Jess isn't much better. Do you know where she is tonight? Is she coming home for dinner?

HARRIET: She called a little earlier. She said she was going out with a friend and not to expect her tonight. She'll probably stay over in town.

REBECCA: I don't know. Ever since she and Michael separated, she seems to have gone wild. She's out all the time. I never know where she is, and she's not pulling her weight around here.

HARRIET: It's been a difficult time for her. It's not easy rebuilding your life after all that she's had to deal with. She lost the baby. She lost Michael, and her job didn't work out. Then she moved in with you and had to come here when you moved in. Lots and lots of changes.

REBECCA: There's no future in cobbling together all those silly little part-time jobs and casual work that she's been doing. She trained for years, and it seems to me that she's thrown all of that away.

HARRIET: Perhaps she needs just a little bit of space and time to sort out what she wants to do with her new life.

REBECCA: Well, I'm not sure how much more time I can give her. I feel like I'm carrying this whole family, and I don't know how much longer I can keep doing it.

HARRIET: I always thought that times were tough when I married your father. You know we couldn't afford a place of our own, and we lived with your grandmother for several years.

REBECCA: (*impatiently*) Yes, I know all those stories. You were still living with Gram when I was born.

HARRIET: And didn't that cause problems? Your grandmother had very strict ideas on how to manage a baby. It was such a relief when we were able to move out into that tiny flat on Ellingham Street. We curtained off part of the hallway to make a bedroom for you.

REBECCA: I don't remember that place but I do remember the flat in Clancy Street where Richard and I shared that single bedroom. I remember Dad made us bunk beds and they were pretty wobbly. I used to be scared that Richard would fall down on top of me.

HARRIET: And then we managed to get enough deposit to buy this place. It felt like a palace to have so much space even though there was such a lot of work to be done to make it liveable. Now, there's still such a lot of work to be done to keep it in good condition.

Jake enters with the tea tray. Tea is served in pretty china cups. He passes the cups to the women, then takes his and sits in his chair.

HARRIET: Thanks, love. I was just saying it will be wonderful when you get time to dig over the vegetable garden and we can grow our own tomatoes and perhaps even try some spinach. (*To Rebecca*) Your father always wanted to grow cauliflowers and never managed it.

REBECCA: I remember one year when he insisted on growing Brussels sprouts and we had to eat them even though they were full of worms. I've never been able to face a Brussels sprout after that year.

HARRIET: They were awful, weren't they? And I had to keep cooking and serving them until they were all gone. He would have been so offended if I told him how much I hated them. Thank goodness he never grew them again.

JAKE: I'll start on it tomorrow. I have to report in to Centrelink in the morning and that can take hours, but I'll make it a priority to start when I get back.

Harriet's phone rings, and she answers it.

HARRIET: It's Jess. Hello darling, how are you? (*silence while she listens*) That would be wonderful. You sure you don't want dinner? (*another silence as she listens to the response*). Alright then, we'll see you after dinner for drinks. (*She looks at Jake*) What time will dinner be ready?

JAKE: It just needs reheating. We should be able to eat in about 20 minutes.

HARRIET: (*on the phone to Jess*) Your dad says we can eat in about 20 minutes, so if you come in about an hour, that will be perfect. Okay, love, see you then. (*She ends the call*). Jess is bringing around with a friend she wants us to meet.

REBECCA: Did she say who this friend is?

HARRIET: No idea she just wants us to meet him.

REBECCA: That sounds interesting.

JAKE: Well, I'd better get dinner organised then.

Jake heaves himself out of his chair, collects the cups, puts them on the tray, and exits with them.

Scene 2

It is now an hour later. The family has finished dinner and is sitting in the lounge with drinks.

JAKE: She should be here any moment. I wonder who this fella is that she's bringing around.

REBECCA: I hope he's an improvement on Michael. I never liked that young man.

JAKE: Not so young now - he has to be in his 40s surely.

REBECCA: And he hasn't aged that well either. I saw him the other day at the corner shop and he's losing his hair.

HARRIET: Well, he's water under the bridge now, and our Jess is better off without him.

JAKE: I ran into Monty the other day and he said Michael was thinking of standing for parliament. I can't say I would want to vote for him. He was always too radical for me.

HARRIET: What do you mean, too radical?

JAKE: He had all these silly ideas. Thought we should close down the immigration detention centres, wanted more subsidies for Green energy and argued that we should increase our income tax bill to improve our health and welfare services. AND he supported the Palestinians. Really!

REBECCA: Improving our health and welfare services doesn't seem like a bad idea to me.

JAKE: You'd be happy to pay more tax?

REBECCA: There must be other ways for governments to raise money. Maybe they should spend less on submarines and weapons.

JAKE: Don't even think about more tax. Please don't even put the idea out there into the universe. (*He crosses his two index fingers and holds them up, then hisses*). We can't afford one more expense right now.

There's a knock at the door. It opens. Jess and Nelson come in. Jess goes to Harriet, leans over, and kisses her cheek.

JESS: Hi Nan (*she turns towards her mother and father*). Mum. Dad. Everyone this is Nelson.

Nelson approaches Harriet first and shakes her hand.

NELSON: Pleased to meet you Mrs. Baxter (*he then approaches Rebecca and Jake and shakes hands with them*) Mrs. Roxon. Nice to meet you Mr. Roxon.

Jess and Nelson sit on the sofa. There is an uneasy silence for a moment.

HARRIET: Can we get you both a drink? What will you have, Jess?

JESS: You're all drinking red. I'm happy to have a red. Nelson?

NELSON: Red is fine by me, thanks.

Rebecca gets up, pours the drinks, and passes them to Jess and Nelson, then sits again.

REBECCA: Cheers.

HARRIET, Jake, Jess and Nelson together: Cheers (*each take a sip*)

HARRIET: So Nelson, tell us a little bit about yourself. Where did you and Jess meet?

NELSON: I run the local auto repair shop. It's been in my family for several generations. My grandfather originally set it up.

JAKE: You mean the garage on the corner of Waverly Street?

NELSON: That's the one

JAKE: Good business?

NELSON: Yeah, okay. Times are getting tough. I can't get enough workers, and I'm having to turn business away. My grandfather would be spinning in his grave at the thought.

REBECCA: What kind of workers are you looking for?

NELSON: I need qualified mechanics and panel beaters. You just can't get decent workers these days. They all want good pay and less hours and they don't have any commitment to the job.

HARRIET: That must be frustrating.

NELSON: It certainly is. I just got rid of my third-year apprentice this morning. He seemed to think it was okay to take a week off work without letting me know and then come in this morning under the influence of some kind of drug. This younger generation seems to think that the world owes them a living, and they're not prepared to work for it.

REBECCA: On the other hand, it's not always easy for young people though, is it? Prices are so high that much of this younger generation will probably never be able to afford to buy their own house and I know a number of my friends' children say they'll never be able to pay off their HECS debt.

JAKE: Something has got to change, doesn't it? There's no work for people like me – people who are willing and able to work. There are not enough tradies and no support to train them. Prices are going through the roof. Inflation is eating up any savings you might have. Mortgage rates are appalling. The cost of electricity is outrageous and we are all struggling to make ends meet.

JESS: I certainly think your generation, mum, and your generation, Nan, have a lot to answer for. The system is broken, and all our current government seem to want to do is fiddle around on the edges and not make the changes that absolutely MUST be made.

REBECCA: Yes, it's pretty depressing with the election coming up to find that none of the major parties seem to be offering any decent options for change. It's all just the same old same old.

NELSON: That's certainly true of the major parties, but have you heard this new bloke? Peter Samuelson? He seems to have some really good ideas.

JAKE: Peter Samuelson? I think I saw something about him on the news the other night. Isn't he that billionaire who made most of his money from coal mining?

NELSON: Yes, that's the one. He's decided to enter politics and he set up a new political party that he called Australians'r'us.

REBECCA: Really? So, what he got to say?

NELSON: There's this great speech on YouTube that he made last week. I think it's worth watching. Mrs Baxter, I see your iPad is sitting there. May I find the clip and show everyone?

HARRIET: Sure.

She passes him the iPad. He finds the clip and this is projected onto the screen at the back of the stage for the audience to see or there is a partial blackout and he presents in person.

PETER SAMUELSON: Our wonderful country is founded on the great Australian dream. In our Australian dream, we all live in our own homes. Homes we can afford. Homes that are comfortable, have space, and, of course, have the great Australian barbie in the backyard. What would we do without the barbie, hey? *(He chuckles)* Australians deserve good healthcare and a decent job followed by a comfortable retirement. We dream of our children having a better life than ours but that dream is not coming true for many Australians. Technology has changed our working lives and the kinds of jobs available. Some traditional jobs are now obsolete. We don't have enough skilled workers for the new industries and professions. Remember when we were kids - the school dropout working in his garage could become a millionaire. Not now. He's lucky to get any work at all.

Our government hands out big tax cuts to the rich whilst the rest of us struggle with smaller minimum wage increases. The rich are getting richer and the poor are falling far behind. Being in the middle class is no longer a feeling of security. More and more of the middle class are falling into poverty and they are paying more tax than many of our richest citizens. The economy should work for everyone, rich and poor alike. The best way to do that is to support the middle class. When the middle class is accessible, the poor are motivated to work to achieve middle-class security. The poor can work hard and get ahead. When people feel their hard work gives them rewards we are all better off. People are busy improving their lives and we don't get the unrest and anger we see today. If you can see wealth and security coming because of your hard work, then you are going to work hard, and the country benefits. We are all better off. You can afford to buy your house, buy nice things to put in it, get your kids the best education, and pay for the best health care. And your lifestyle supports all those retail workers, manufacturers, tradespeople, and professionals who provide the goods and services you and your family consume.

At the level of government, we need to operate within our budget. Households should not go into debt and nor should the government. We cannot operate in deficit. We need to create more jobs for people. We need people to be healthy so they can work and improve their lives so that means better healthcare.

We can't let political games and posturing get in our way. We can make things better for many people if we just get on with the job instead of playing games. We are aiming for all the things Australia stands for good jobs with good pay, good education for our kids, a home of our own, a good healthcare system you can rely on, a secure retirement, and opportunities for those who want to work to succeed. Australians'r'us will work for all of these things. We are not part of today's corrupt system. We are a breath of fresh air that will sweep through Australian politics and make things better for all Australians. Australia needs a strong hand at the helm, a strong leader who will take no bullshit and work for what we need to turn this country around. I am such a leader; a strongman. On election day, vote for Peter Samuelson and Australians'r'us!

Lights up

JAKE: That makes a lot of sense.

NELSON: Yes, I really like what he has to say. He's got a candidate from his party in our electorate. Dr. Martin Gurney. I was thinking of volunteering to help with his campaign.

JESS: Are you sure that's a good idea? You're incredibly busy with the business? When will you have time?

NELSON: It seems to me that his ideas will create lots of space for the business to grow so I figure it's worth the time now.

REBECCA: There's no doubt the rhetoric sounds great, but I don't hear any practical actions suggested. How is he going to do what he says he wants to do?

NELSON: The government we have now has made so many mistakes, and the impact has been devastating for ordinary Australians. I think we've got to a point where people are not going to take it any longer. Politicians are liars and cheaters and fraudsters and they are destroying our country.

REBECCA: Well, given all the recent media reports on corruption, abuse of power and people, it's hard to argue against that, but I would still like to see our candidates providing realistic solutions to the problems we face. It's easy to talk ideas. It's much harder to implement sound strategies.

JESS: Mum, you're always so negative. This guy is saying all the right things. Why don't you give him a chance?

REBECCA: I guess time will tell. Let's not argue about politics here. Let me top up your glasses.

PETER SAMUELSON: Politicians are phoneys and charlatans. Vote for honesty. Vote for Peter Samuelson.

Scene 3

PETER SAMUELSON: What a wonderful day for Australia. For the first time in our political history, we have a party for the people voted into Parliament. Australians'r'us is a party of the people and for the people: you, the ordinary everyday citizens of Australia. We are you. We are regular, ordinary, everyday Australians just like you. And just like you, we want our country to be great. Now it's time for all Australians to get together and work together to rebuild this great nation of ours. I will be a Prime Minister for all Australians. I understand you all did not vote for me (*chuckles*), but that's okay. I understand. Some of you have been fooled by the fake swindlers who have been running our country up until now. Their control over the media, saturated with left-wing churnalists, means that all you hear is fake news and untruths. I have news for you all. Times have changed. No more fake news churnalism. You will hear the truth from me and from Parliament, and we will make sure that the media reports us fairly and accurately.

Now that I am your prime minister, I hope that we can all work together. After all, we all want the same things: good jobs for all, a good standard of living, a healthy life, good opportunities for our children, and a secure retirement. Our party consists of Australians from all backgrounds who want their government to serve the people. We have wonderful people who epitomise how to succeed through hard work. Our people have worked and built their own businesses through their own grit and determination. They have shown us all how to succeed in these uncertain times. They have already shown us by their own examples how hard work creates success and provides employment opportunities for others. We have wonderful people who are committed to working hard to serve you, the people. And serve the people we will. It is time we all worked together to rebuild our wonderful nation. We want to make sure you are all involved. We don't want anyone to miss out.

We have a plan. We need to focus on the economy. We need to increase our growth rates and aim to have the best economy in the world. We will be respected partners in international affairs: we are happy to get along with anyone as long as they make an effort to get along with us. We won't take any nonsense from anybody. Relationships are two-way streets. You scratch my back, I'll scratch yours. You become obstructive I'll turn my back on you. I'm a reasonable man. I won't take crap from anyone. Don't get in my way. I can be your best friend, or I can be your worst enemy. Your choice. Our wonderful country needs to stand tall, be respected. We win respect by standing strong – not giving in to tyrants and dictators. We won't be bullied. You don't play ball with us, then you can take your goods somewhere else – we will manage without you. Agree with us, and we will be your best friend. Don't play ball and we will show you we can manage without you. No trade agreement is worth surrendering our self-respect. No treaty is worth our citizens fighting your wars. Look after your own trouble.

We are keen to get started. We will rebuild our economy. We will make sure all those who want to work have jobs that pay them a decent wage. We will make sure that our industry and business sectors can grow unobstructed – we know that growth creates jobs. Let industry and business grow and develop. Let's make things here and sell them here. Let's create new industries and stop exporting our greatest achievements. Let the wealth created by growth be shared with regular, ordinary Australians through employment growth. Let us face the challenges, and we will solve them and get on with making our country great. We are not frightened of hard work. We will get the job done. Our work is only just beginning and we will keep going till it is done. You will be proud to be Australian once again.

Scene 4

The Baxter's living room the morning after the election. Harriet is knitting. Jess and Nelson are sitting on the sofa. Jake is sprawled in a lounge chair. Rebecca comes in with the tea tray and hands everyone a cup of tea using the pretty bone china cups.

REBECCA: That's right, isn't it? No milk for you, Nelson. And mum. I've sugared yours.

NELSON: Thanks, Mrs. Roxton.

REBECCA: I'm sorry lunch today was only a casserole. The price of meat these days is outrageous, and I couldn't find a roast for anything under $30 that would feed us all.

PETER SAMUELSON: Just eaten a wonderful wagyu steak to celebrate victory. Best $250 I've spent this week. And all Australian. You know, we have the best in the world. Australia is great.

HARRIET: Sunday roast is such a tradition. I remember fighting with my brother to scrape the remains of the Yorkshire pudding out of the fat in the roasting dish. It was more delicious the longer it soaked in the meat fat.

JAKE: I can't remember the last time we had a roast.

JESS: We had roast chicken just the other night.

HARRIET: No, a Sunday roast is supposed to be Lamb or beef, not chicken.

REBECCA: Well, chickens are about the only meat we can afford to eat these days. Did you see the price of steak at the supermarket on Friday? It was over $35 a kilo. How can anyone afford that?

HARRIET: It's a sad state of affairs when we can't afford to eat the way we always have done in the past. Not that there's anything wrong with your casserole, Rebecca love, it was very nice.

REBECCA: Padded out with a multitude of vegetables. I am having to make the smallest cuts of meat go further and further. (*pause*) While I think of it, Jess, I couldn't get the ham you wanted for your sandwiches for lunch. I just didn't have enough money. I'm sorry.

JESS: That's okay, mum. I'll make do. My friend Charlene has a whole lot of tomatoes she bought into work on Friday and I grabbed a few. Her tomato plants were really successful this year.

HARRIET: I can remember making tomato sauce and tomato chutney from our tomatoes. I did it for years and years. Maybe we can do it again next year when your father gets the garden organised.

JAKE: The freezer is busted and we can't afford to fix it or replace it.

HARRIET: That's okay – we can bottle things.

REBECCA: I remember those weekend working bees where you had us stirring the chutney and bottling the tomatoes. I haven't done that for years.

HARRIET: It will save us some money if we have those preserves. And I think if we look in the storage cupboard under the house, we will find a whole pile of preserving jars. I wonder if we can still get the seals.

JESS: We can get just about anything on eBay so if we can't get any here we can order some online. I think I remember from when I was a very small child you doing some bottling mum. But I have no idea how to do it now.

REBECCA: Yes, I haven't done any for years but I used to cook up the apples from that huge tree we had in the back garden and bottle those. You always wanted something sweet after dinner and you would have the puréed apples with ice cream.

JESS: No desserts for us these days, which isn't a bad thing for our waistlines

PETER SAMUELSON: Feeding the starving only increases their hunger. They need to work for their food.

JAKE: (*to Nelson*) You must be very pleased with the election results. Martin Gurney won in our electorate by a landslide. Peter Samuelson will be our new prime minister. Who would've thought that 12 months ago - what a success story.

NELSON: Yes, it was an amazing celebration last night. Martin was over the moon, and Peter Samuelson's victory speech blew us all out of the water. We have a great future ahead of us.

REBECCA: I certainly hope so, but I still don't see a lot of clear action plans.

JESS: Oh, mum, how can you be so negative?

REBECCA: I'm not being negative. I think what they are saying sounds wonderful but I would really like to know what it is they are actually going to do.

NELSON: Peter Samuelson was clear. They are going to kickstart the economy.

REBECCA: Yes, I heard that, but how are they going to do that?

NELSON: He will have some really clever plans ready to implement, I'm sure. I don't understand economics so I don't know what would work but Peter and his colleagues do.

PETER SAMUELSON: Tax cuts for business and a reduction in regulatory burden.

REBECCA: I certainly hope so. I'm not sure how much longer we can hang on even with us all sharing the house. The expenses are huge and it's really only my income and a little bit of Jess's that keeps us going.

NELSON: Things should turn around very quickly. I certainly hope so. The business is struggling because I just can't get decent workers. I'm thinking I might have to sell my house and put the money into the business to keep it going until things get better.

JESS: Well, if necessary, you can always move in with us.

NELSON: Thanks, babe. I hope it won't come to that.

JESS: Are you saying you don't want to live with me?

NELSON: No absolutely not but I would like us to stand on our own 2 feet and not be dependent on your family.

JAKE: That's understandable.

HARRIET: Well, the house is big enough, and you are welcome. If it gets to that, in this brave new world, I would like to think the new government will look at the healthcare system. I have not been able to see a doctor for months. I need my prescriptions renewed, but there are no doctors left at my surgery, and we have to make telehealth appointments. After my last one, I found out that because I have not seen a doctor face-to-face in the last 6 months, I am no longer eligible for Medicare on my telehealth appointments. I don't know how I am going to pay for the appointment; I need to get my next prescription renewal.

REBECCA: That sucks. It's not your fault there are no doctors in town, and you have to use telehealth.

PETER SAMUELSON: Major cuts to Medicare needed to cover reduced tax income from business and industry. Lower-income thresholds for free healthcare.

JAKE: I would like to see an increase in employment opportunities. And maybe training schemes that will accept workers of my age to retrain to where the need is greatest.

REBECCA: I would just like a change in work culture where the bosses focus on the well-being of their staff and not solely on the bottom line. I'm sick of being disrespected and treated like a piece of shit under the boss's boot.

JESS: You think you've got it bad? You ought to try being a casual at the very bottom of the totem pole. I'm lucky if I get treated like a human being rather than an uneducated animal.

HARRIET: Do you think it's worth thinking about trying to go back to your career instead of taking all these part-time casual jobs?

JESS: Maybe I will one day, but right now, I still feel too burned out to even consider going back. I know the longer I am out, the more dated my experience gets. It's a catch-22.

JAKE: I'll never get back into my profession – technology has changed things so much, and I just haven't been able to keep up. I'd be happy with any old job that didn't have me standing on my feet all day.

NELSON: Well, we are at the beginning of a new era, and we all hope that things will get better for us. The sooner, the better. Let's raise a glass, or rather a cuppa, to Peter Samuelson, the strongman.

They all raise their cups and chorus, "Cheers."

PETER SAMUELSON: Say it often enough and loud enough and they will believe you: Things are going to get better. Things are going to get better. Things are going to get better.

Scene 5

The scene opens to the empty lounge room a year later. Rebecca comes in supporting Harriet who is very shaky on her feet. She settles Harriet into an armchair.

REBECCA: There you go, mum. Jake will be in in a minute with your cuppa.

HARRIET: Thanks, love

Harriet picks up her knitting, which is beside her chair on a small table, and starts to knit. Rebecca sits in her chair. Jake enters with the tea tray, followed by Jess and Nelson. They all sit. Jake hands out the tea in the pretty china cups.

NELSON: Thanks for dinner, Mrs. Roxon.

JESS: I don't know how you managed to make a yummy dinner out of that small amount of leftovers, mum. You're incredible.

REBECCA: I'm glad it tasted okay. I was a little worried, but having the tomatoes we preserved this year has really helped.

JESS: It would have been a lot easier if the freezer hadn't died on us! It was certainly a team effort getting all of those bottles done. I didn't remember it being such hard work.

REBECCA: Well, the last time we did it, you were only a small child and spent more time playing than helping out.

NELSON: It's clearly an important skill and more people should learn how to do it.

HARRIET: All the things I did when I first married now seem to be coming back. We didn't have freezers, and I don't remember buying tinned food when you kids were little. I DO remember -intimately - the ptomaine poisoning scare that really put lots of people off preserving fruit and vegetables. I've never felt so rotten. It was about then that it was easier to get tinned stuff.

JESS: I'm glad I didn't know about that before eating our preserves.

HARRIET: It's just a matter of sealing the jars properly.

REBECCA: I always check. It's fine.

NELSON: It's nearly time for the big address. Can I set it up for us on the iPad?

Harriet passes over the iPad, and Nelson sets up the address.

JAKE: It's hard to believe it's been 12 months since the election. I must admit I'm a little disappointed at the progress this new government has made.

REBECCA: It doesn't surprise me

Harriet puts her hand to her head and seems to be swaying. Rebecca glances over sees her mother jumps up and goes to stand by her with her hand on her shoulder.

REBECCA: Mum, are you okay?

HARRIET: It's alright, dear. I just feel a little faint. I'll be fine.

The two remain in position for a minute, and then Harriet starts to breathe easier. She sits up straighter and smiles at Rebecca.

HARRIET: It's over now. I'm fine.

REBECCA: You really haven't seemed very well these last few months, mum. Is there something we should know?

HARRIET: Nothing to worry about love. I'm just getting old, and my body is starting to wear out.

REBECCA: What does your doctor say?

HARRIET: (vague and dismissive) Oh, he's fine with me.

REBECCA: Mum, I'm …….

Nelson interrupts.

NELSON: It's time.

As before, the speech can be either projected and pre-recorded, or the lights can drop, and the speech comes from in front of the curtain.

PETER SAMUELSON: Greetings to my fellow Australians. Thank you, thank you, thank you for your support over the last year. We all know it's been a really difficult year. We're starting to lay the foundation of sound economic growth but there are trends that have been building for decades that are so difficult to overturn. Trends like this winner-takes-all economy where the rich get richer, and everybody else struggles not to drown. Those trends are very difficult to overturn, and they have been made worse by current international problems. We know the situation in Israel. They need to go in there and just get it over and done with. We don't want the radical revolution spreading to our wonderful country. Stop it in its tracks. Keep it over there, and don't come our way. We don't want you. Just do as I say and get it over with.

Our last government did nothing to address these problems, rather they made them worse. Look at how they handled the situation in Yemen. Appalling. Supporting those jihadist terrorists. We don't want them. We don't want anything to do with them. Don't let them into our country claiming to be victims. Taking our resources and stealing our jobs. Don't let them poison the blood of our country. Lock them up in detention centres then send them back to where they came from. They are not people. They are animals. Treat them like the animals they are. And any of you who agree with them. Leave. Go where you are wanted. You are vermin, and we will eradicate you without mercy.

And now those power-hungry dumbwits are no longer in power, those in the past government, the so-called opposition, continue to work against us, blocking our efforts to drive change. The past government has spent wildly, totally out-of-control, leaving our economy in a perilous state. We all know what happens when you spend madly. We are heading into a recession. Interest rates are going up. Unemployment rates are going up. And it's all their fault. They should not have been left in charge of a piggy bank. We all know the consequences of spending more than we earn. The past government never learned this lesson and continues to lobby us to increase funding in all kinds of areas. Why should we spend more on healthcare as the bleeding hearts keep demanding? How can increased funding in healthcare benefit our economy? A few jobs for healthcare workers? No. Get off the gravy train and get a real job. A job where you earn a living by the sweat of your brow. Why should we increase the unemployment benefit? Those trendy lefties cannot explain to me how paying people more to stay at home and not work can possibly benefit our economy. Surely, even a dumb child can see how that does not work. If you don't work, you don't deserve a decent income. And why should we send our troops overseas to fight someone else's battles? Pftt! Treaties? I spit on treaties that don't benefit us. Let us look after our own before we worry about someone else. It's our country and our lives.

Be wise. Don't believe the crap coming out of their mouths. It's fake news. What they are saying, what you are reading about them, it's not true. They are liars. They mismanaged the economy for decades, and now we are all paying for that. It is a terrible path they have put our feet on, and we can only reverse that if we treat them in the same way. I will make sure ASIO investigates them all. Their corruption will come to light, and they will be prosecuted without mercy. Lock them up. Throw away the key. Hey, maybe we can invest in some floating prisons; being rocked all day in a windowless cabin below the water level sounds like a fair punishment to me – and then forgotten about forever. Never to see the light of day again. Hmm. Worth thinking about.

But back to business. We need to support businesses and industries in creating jobs. We don't need a short-term fix. We need a long-term plan based on a steady, consistent effort to reverse the disasters promulgated by previous governments. Their criminal mismanagement. The choices we make are not just going to determine what happens to young people today but impact the following generations. The choices we make today will shape our future. The choices I make are really THAT important. The world is not going to shift and go back in time. We live in a global world that uses technology, and that is not going to go away. We have to find ways to make them work for us. We don't want to give up and resign ourselves to lower living standards. We need to work together and fight back. We need to invest in education so that our children grow up to be workers who are competitive internationally. We need to rethink our education system so our kids graduate with real world skills. We need businesses and industry to work in partnership with education; we need industry and business to tell the schools what skills students need. They need to be involved in designing the curriculum so that when students graduate, they know they have a job waiting for them. Employers need to be sure that their workers can do the work. They don't need wishy-washy trendy-lefties. They need practical, sensible workers who can get on with the job and not waste their time arguing about stuff that is none of their business. Heads down, work, work, work is what we need people to do. Less time mealy-mouthing off about fairness and equity and all that rubbish and more focus on just getting on with it. We need industry and business to be given sufficient flexibility to grow and create new jobs. We need to get rid of the outrageous rules that restrict how businesses operate and put more emphasis on making the profits needed to fuel growth. We need to stop investing in green dreams that are costing us a fortune and get back to good old basics – coal-fired electricity will see our energy needs met for a good time to come, and we already have the infrastructure – we don't need to waste money on building those costly alternatives. We reject stupid, woke ideology. We need to dismantle diversity, equity, and inclusion programs – programs that just support the few who can't cut the mustard anyway, and focus more on the average, everyday worker, who can do the job, do it well, and do it consistently. When business and industry are healthy, employment is healthy. When employment is healthy, people can work hard, earn money, and be better off.

We need to manage the deficit we inherited from the previous government. Those incompetent, bungling criminals. Throttlebottoms all. Isn't that a wonderful word? Go and look it up. It's my word of the day. Those throttle-bottoms shouldn't have been put in charge of a piggy bank, let alone the finances of our wonderful country. Bet none of them can even balance their own cheque books. Ha, ha. Bet they are too dumb to even know that cheque books are out, and it's all plastic money now. Boy, I'd hate to have to pay their credit card bills. Hmm, I wonder what a helicopter to my electorate would cost. Better check it out.

Yes, I know it is hard now. Regular, everyday Australians are doing it tough. Why, just the other day, one of my electorate told me they had to cut back on eating out to only 3 nights a week. Imagine that! And I hear that some are even selling their third car and making do with two. Whew!

And don't get me started on the Greens and their push for electric. How can you tow your caravan with an electric car? Where is the oomph! We'd have to do a Fred Flintstone and get out and push. That would be funny. And don't get me started on what the farmers think of electric utes. Can you imagine an electric tractor? No harvesting the wheat if it's not a sunny day, hey! No bread in the shops today love because it was overcast last week. (*he chuckles – clearly very amused by his joke*)

I promise our economy will get better and it will be stronger each year. We will go back to basics. I have two years left in my prime ministership, and I intend to spend every second of that time making sure I do what has to be done so that ordinary, everyday families, working families, and people who are struggling every single day know that work can lead them to a better place. We will overcome the legacy left by the fraudsters and cheats and build a new Australia. An Australia that will grow from strength to strength. Thank you for your support, and let's keep working together.

Lights up

NELSON: I don't think he realised just how bad things were in Canberra and with the budget before he won the election.

JAKE: I'd certainly like to have seen more progress around employment. I understand the government don't want to keep paying unemployment benefits when people are not making the effort to look for work but I have never stopped trying and they're now talking of reducing my benefit because I have been unemployed for a long time.

REBECCA: You're kidding me. We are struggling to manage as it is. How can we manage on less income?

JAKE: I'm trying love.

Rebecca smiles at him but continues to look worried. Jake stares at the floor. Harriet hunches over, apparently in pain, but no one notices her. After a few moments she sits back up and continues to knit.

NELSON: I'm hoping the changes in TAFE education will get me a couple of apprentices. I just cannot get staff, and I hate turning work away. You know, poor Mrs. Riley has been waiting six months to get some work done on her car, and because it's not super urgent, I just can't get to it.

REBECCA: It seems no one can get enough staff. I was on the phone for two hours last week trying to get some information from the Council about the rates for this house. It's hopeless.

JAKE: (*he sounds defeated, flat*) You ought to try the check-in system for the unemployment benefit. It's all AI run and God help you if you want to do anything other than the bog standard. It just ties you up in endless loops, and you get absolutely nowhere.

JESS: You're telling me. I had to call Nelson's insurance company for that vandalism at the garage last month, and the process was an absolute nightmare. It seemed nothing happened unless I managed to get a hold of a real person to talk to, but each time I called, there was a minimum of an hour's wait to get to a real person. They kept saying you can do this online but when I sent an online enquiry, I never got a response at all.

JAKE: It certainly seems I trained for the wrong job when I was a kid. If I'd trained as a panel beater or a mechanic I could be working with you now Nelson. Bit late now, ay?

NELSON: If I could take you on, Jake, I would, but business is so tight at the moment. Costs have gone up exponentially, wages have gone up but income has not.

Jake looks up hopefully towards Rebecca, but she is engaged with Nelson and Jess and does not notice. After a pause, he slumps down in his chair again, appearing to disengage.

HARRIET: (*pauses her knitting and speaking in a wavering, uncertain voice*) My pension hasn't gone up for 10 years. I just wish costs hadn't gone up in that time, either. And I'd love to see a real human Doctor for a change.

No one is paying attention to her. She waits for a response but, not getting one, looks down and continues to knit.

REBECCA: Talking of costs, Jake, did you manage to fix that leaking tap this morning? The council increased our water rates by over 60% this year, so we can't afford to waste even the smallest drop.

JAKE: (*sits more upright and speaks more brightly than before*) Yes, I had a look at it, and I've replaced the washer, but it's really only a temporary fix. The tap itself is so old it's worn out and we will need to replace it in the near future.

REBECCA: Oh God, another expense.

JAKE: I'll have a good search online - sometimes you can get stuff from China that's a lot cheaper than what you can find here.

REBECCA: Fingers crossed it fits. Goodness knows how old the pipes are. Have pipes changed their size over the years?

JAKE: I have absolutely no idea. I can only look.

JESS: And there goes another job for an Australian worker - you're buying stuff from overseas.

Jake flinches at the criticism, but no one notices. He hunches down in his chair again.

REBECCA: Not like we have much choice.

PETER SAMUELSON: From today, there will be an increase in tariffs for Chinese goods and a further tax cut for big businesses. We need to buy Australian and generate Australian jobs.

JESS: Well, do as the Man said. Do the hard yards now, and things will get better.

REBECCA: They may well get better, but between now and then, I still need to eat, and it's getting to the point where even that is problematic.

Harriet drops her knitting and begins to cough and gasp for breath. She bends over in her chair. Rebecca rushes to her side lights go down.

Scene 6

Lights come up on the same lounge room. It is empty. Rebecca and Jake enter. They are dressed in black.

JAKE: That was a lovely funeral service. Your mother would have been very pleased.

REBECCA: I still feel so guilty. She deserved better than a cardboard coffin and a pathetically small wreath.

Jess enters as Rebecca is speaking. She is also in black.

JESS: Oh, mum, don't be so old-fashioned. Cardboard coffins are ever so much more sustainable and really, really popular now. Nan would not have cared, but for those of us left behind, it's a much better option for the environment. And the wreath was lovely. Size doesn't matter.

NELSON: (*entering as Jess finishes - he is in jeans and an open-necked shirt*) Size doesn't matter? Really babe, not sure this is appropriate conversation for the occasion.

REBECCA: (*scornfully*) Dickhead. (*She sits down*)

PETER SAMUELSON: I don't believe in this climate change nonsense. Look at how clean our air and water are. Then, look at the air in China, South East Asia, and parts of South America. It's so dirty. And the oceans are so small. Look at how much rubbish from Asia we pick off our beaches every year. It just washes down in the Pacific. It just washes down.

REBECCA: It was lovely that the church ladies put on some food after the service. We could never have afforded to feed all the people who turned up.

JAKE: It was a surprise how popular your mother actually was. I didn't expect that number of people at her funeral. We certainly did not see them visit her in her last months.

REBECCA: Mum was really proud. I don't think many people knew how sick she was. She used to be really engaged in a lot of community work. She did a lot of home visiting when we had that influx of refugees about 10 years ago. She used to help out in the Information Centre. She was really active in the Gardening group and until the last few months, she did one morning a week at the local Vinnies store.

NELSON: I've noticed with a number of my older clients when I mention I'm living here with you their response is invariably: "Oh you mean with Harriet?" She was really well known - a very special person.

JESS: I know the doctor insisted on an autopsy. Do we have the results? Do we actually know what happened to Nan?

REBECCA: Yes, I spoke to the nurse practitioner at her doctor's surgery. It seems that mum stopped taking her medication 6 months ago. I remember her saying that because she hadn't seen a doctor face-to-face for six months, the rules meant that she could not claim Medicare for her telehealth appointments, so she stopped getting prescriptions renewed when they ran out. I wish I had known. I would have done anything to get the money for her so she could get her prescriptions renewed, but she never said anything, and it never occurred to me to check on her.

JESS: You mean she stopped her medication because she couldn't afford the doctor's appointment, and she couldn't afford it because she had to use telehealth because there were no doctors at her surgery?

JAKE: That's appalling! I didn't realise that.

REBECCA: And it gets worse. Because of the shortage of doctors, surgeries are now saying that if you have not seen a doctor face-to-face in six months, you get dropped off their books, and you do not have a GP at all. There are no new doctors coming into town opening their lists for you to get a new GP. That means that no one in this family currently has access to a GP – not even one via telehealth – so nobody better get sick.

PETER SAMUELSON: We need to make Medicare less expensive. Do you know we spend over 10% of GDP on healthcare in this country? Over 10%. It's too much. People need to take responsibility for their own heath. If they get sick, let them pay. The government can't keep bailing them out.

JESS: But I need the contraceptive pill.

REBECCA: Well, you're not going to get one. You'll have to use something that doesn't need a prescription.

NELSON: Aren't there some overseas places where you can get medication without a prescription? I know some of my customers talk about ordering their medication overseas and having it sent here. They say it's much cheaper and it's easy to access.

REBECCA: That's possible, but the rules around quality control can be very different, and that can be quite risky.

JESS: I'm about due for a new prescription, so I'll have to figure something out.

REBECCA: (*sarcastically*) I notice our prime minister has refused to address the lack of funding in our healthcare system. Clearly, it is not one of his priorities in his claim to rebuild our economic system. Maybe it's his secret agenda to rebuild the economic system by reducing the population. Lots of us are going to die off without access to medical care.

NELSON: That's hardly fair. He can't do everything at once.

REBECCA: He's got the money to reduce taxes for big businesses. Maybe if he taxed them, that funding could go into the healthcare system.

NELSON: But big business needs stimulus to grow, and that growth will create jobs.

REBECCA: And those jobs won't be filled if we're all sick and dead.

JESS: You're being unreasonable mum. Employment is a key driver of our economy and we must make sure there are jobs for all before things can improve.

REBECCA: As I said, if there are fewer people then we need fewer jobs to employ them all so let's just let them die off and all will be fine.

JESS: Oh mum, you're being silly.

Lights down

Act two - Scene 7

We are in the open-plan living area of a small flat. Some of the furniture from Act 1 is there, including the two old lounge chairs, but no sofa. There is a dining table (too large for the space) with two chairs upstage. Everything is old and battered. Throughout this act, the actors' clothes become increasingly shabby. Rebecca enters. She is dressed in old jeans, grubby trainers, and a shabby sweater. She is carrying a cup of tea in an old mug. She throws herself down onto one of the armchairs. Jake comes in a few moments later, carrying a mug of tea. He puts his mug down carefully on the floor beside his chair and then sits down.

JAKE: What time do you have to start work tonight?

REBECCA: I'm getting picked up at seven. Mary is a darling and is happy to pick me up for my shift. We're cleaning at that new office building in the centre of town tonight. It's all glass and that stuff is so hard to clean. I hate it.

JAKE: You could try going back to teaching.

REBECCA: (*laughs bitterly*). Not an option after the way I left my post last year. I'll not get another job teaching around here, that's for sure.

JAKE: Accusing your boss of sexual harassment doesn't earn you any brownie points.

REBECCA: And none of the other staff stood up for me. They were all too scared of him, so I come off looking like a troublemaker. Anyway, I don't want to go back to teaching. The curriculum has been changed so much over the last two years. I don't like what we are required to teach the kids; it's very one-sided and biased. Kids are not encouraged to think for themselves anymore.

JAKE: The promised shake-up of the education system seems to be focused on producing drones who cannot think for themselves.

REBECCA: It's destroyed me, being part of that. I know we could do with the money, but I just cannot bring myself to teach that shit.

PETER SAMUELSON: It is time this government abolished the Departments of Education in each of the states and territories and took over federally. The states have made a right mess of education – look at the disparities in curriculum, school starting ages, and school holidays across the country. If parents can't move their kids from one school to another in a different state without disadvantaging their child's learning, then clearly something has to be done. We will save a fortune in funding by not reinventing the education wheel in each state and territory. Our Federal Bureau of Education will be much more efficient and cost-effective, leading to a better quality of education across the nation. We will establish a standardised federal curriculum that schools must follow if they want any government funding. We want to ensure our children finish schools with the right skills for the job market. We will establish citizenship education into the curriculum – our children need to understand what patriotism is and how to become patriotic citizens of our wonderful nation. We will require the 10 Commandments to be posted in every classroom. Our children need to learn how to behave morally; their moral development is key to good citizenship. We will commission standardised textbooks to be used across the entire nation and a week-by-week series of lesson plans in all subject areas that ensure that all our children are learning the same things at the same time. This will be such a benefit for our families who move inter-state – their children can walk out of one classroom one day and into another in a different state the next day, and their education is not interrupted – they can keep on learning.

We need teachers who are good at their jobs. Teachers whose students get good results in NAPLAN testing will be able to advance their careers – teachers whose students perform poorly in NAPLAN will be required to undergo compulsory retraining at their own expense in order to improve their skills. We are no longer going to reward schools whose student performances are poor. Additional funding for so-called disadvantaged schools will be cut immediately. Teachers are the most important factor shaping student success, and it is no longer acceptable for teachers to blame students for their own laziness and poor performance.

We will take a back-to-basics approach, and we will have the best education system in the world. Our graduates will get jobs and contribute to our economy and prosperity.

Rebecca notices a paper on the floor and reaches down to pick it up - it's all screwed up. She smooths it out

REBECCA: What's this?

JAKE: (*looks away*) They're going to cut my bloody benefit again. They've lowered the threshold of family income of eligibility for the unemployment benefit.

REBECCA: You're kidding.

Jake: I know. Haven't you listened to the politicians? Our Prime Minister clearly stated when he was re-elected that we unemployed are lazy louts, happy to sit at home and do nothing while we claim the benefit so the obvious solution is to reduce the benefit well below poverty line so that even the lowest paying job will pay better than the benefit.

PETER SAMUELSON: People are taking advantage of the welfare system. We can't allow that. Success comes from hard work, not bludging off the government.

REBECCA: I keep hoping that you will qualify for the old age pension, but they keep increasing the age for that as well.

JAKE: Yes, two years ago I would have been able to claim the benefit this year, but now I have another three years before I'm eligible.

REBECCA: I could try and get you a job on one of the cleaning teams. The pay's awful but it will be a little better than what you will be getting on your benefit.

JAKE: I guess. It's hard to think that a few years ago, I was working in those fancy buildings downtown, and now I probably can't even get a job cleaning them at night.

REBECCA: I really miss the garden at mum's old place. You were able to grow lots of vegetables and fruit and preserving them really helped us get through the winter months. Here we can't even have pot plants let alone grow anything useful.

JAKE: The concessions your mum got because she was on the old age pension made it possible for us all to live there. We lost all of those when she died.

REBECCA: The rates bill alone was phenomenal, and I know the council put in an application for a 50% rate rise just after we sold the place. We could never have paid that even with the most generous payment plan the council would agree to. It seems we are punished for living in an area where the local council has mismanaged our money for decades. It's not fair. I bet people in the cities don't pay the huge rates that we did.

PETER SAMUELSON: I wonder how much we could save if we abolished the cumbersome triple tier government system we have here in Australia? Do we really need federal, state and local governments? One federal government would be much more cost effective.

JAKE: And then we went and put a lot of money into Nelson's business to keep it afloat. What a mistake that was. Now, even this place costs more in rent than we can really afford.

REBECCA: We didn't really have a choice. Without a car and the increase in public transport fees, we needed to live close enough to town for me to walk to work.

Jake sighs and looks down. Rebecca fiddles with her mug. There is a short silence. Then, there is a knock on the door. Nelson and Jess enter. They both grab a dining table chair and bring them in to sit near Rebecca and Jake.

JESS: Are you on the team that's cleaning that new office building tonight, mum?

REBECCA: Yes.

JESS: I've been asked to fill in for Stacey on your team tonight. Is there anything I should know about this job?

REBECCA: It's all stainless steel and glass. It's a bastard to polish, and it will be worse tonight because it's school holidays. Mr. Johansson has his kids in the office for some of the time, and you wouldn't believe the sticky fingerprints all over the glass. It's a nightmare.

JESS: So, not just an easy vacuum, dust, and empty the rubbish?

REBECCA: Absolutely not. Make yourself a cuppa if you like love. The teabags in the sink have only been used once, so they can be used again.

JESS: No, it's fine, thanks Mum.

JAKE: (*somewhat sarcastically*) How's the business going, Nelson, or shouldn't I ask?

NELSON: Things are really tight. I've had to lay off a couple of staff. People are just not getting their cars fixed and the insurance jobs are demanding tighter and tighter budgets. It's almost not worth doing an insurance fix. They have cut the overheads so much that I can't cover the cost of the workers' wages to do an insurance job let alone the cost of overheads like electricity and water.

JESS: A couple of those big insurance companies are nightmares to work with. They question every little expense. We submitted a quote the other day that had to be itemised in such detail the quote was 10 pages long. I swear every screw had to be listed.

NELSON: I really appreciate that you have stepped in to do the reception and office work. I know how tired you are, particularly when you pick up extra cleaning shifts at night.

JESS: Well, I didn't have much choice. We need to live close to your work so that we can both walk to work and it's lovely that mum and dad have a flat in the same block so we can keep seeing each other regularly. How are things with you dad?

Jake shrugs and looks down.

PETER SAMUELSON: We are an aging population. Did you know the percentage of older Australians in our population has more than doubled in the last 50 years? We can't afford to carry the heavy financial burden generated by our overly generous welfare system for pensioners. Our citizens need to be productive. They need to generate their own income and not bludge off the state.

JAKE: They're cutting my bloody pension again. Maybe I should try some cleaning shifts with your mother.

JESS: I'm not sure how you will manage that kind of physical work with your heart condition, dad. What does your doctor say?

JAKE: What bloody Doctor? I don't have one.

JESS: (*alarmed*) But surely you have to get your heart medication renewed regularly. Who does that? And when did you have your last check-up?

JAKE: I can get the pills I need from overseas and don't need a prescription, so I'm just continuing to take what I have done for the last few years. It's fine.

REBECCA: It's not fine, but we don't have any other options. Your dad is on the waiting list at the hospital for a check-up, but he is not considered urgent and the last time I checked the waiting list was over two years long and it keeps growing.

JESS: We came here to tell you some news (*she reaches over to hold Nelson's hand*). We are pregnant.

REBECCA: Jess! Are you okay about that?

NELSON: I don't know how we're going to manage financially, but having a baby with Jess is wonderful.

JESS: It's kind of scary. I can organise a playpen to have the baby with me at Nelson's work, but if I'm going to carry on the cleaning shifts at night, Nelson will have to babysit.

REBECCA: Perhaps Nelson can take on the cleaning shifts at night so you are there to do the night feeds with the baby.

JESS: It's worth thinking about but Nelson works physically all day so he's really tired by the evening. At least in the office I'm sitting down for most of the day.

Jake grunts, Nelson looks smug.

REBECCA: *(sarcastically)* Well, we're all waiting for this economic upturn that we have been promised. In a perfect world, we will see some change between now and when the baby is born. Fingers crossed.

PETER SAMUELSON: You know, I am sick of hearing all these climate change nellies going on and on. The risks associated with climate change are negligible compared to the problems we face righting the economy. My scientists are clear that sea level rises will be less than a centimeter over the next 300 years. That is nothing. Why are we wasting time on this rubbish? Air quality is actually improving, so why do we need to cut back on greenhouse gasses? Australia emits less than 1% of global greenhouse gasses. Less than 1%. So why are we making such a fuss about this? We need to withdraw from the Paris Agreement and make sure that every new regulation we endorse in this area is matched by a withdrawal of TWO, yes TWO, related policies. We need the energy generated by our power plants, and we cannot stifle their important work because of the shameful and outrageous limits placed on them. We have a number of fully functioning coal-fired plants that are generating perfectly well. Yes, they have a limited life span, and we have plans to replace each and every one of them when they reach the end of their life span, which isn't for quite some time yet. But when the time comes, we will replace them with small nuclear power-generating plants. Now, that might sound radical and scary, but think about it. For years, we have been frightened by academics who focus on the problems and the risks of nuclear power. It's time we start listening to the politicians who recognize the potential for long-term, efficient, and economical generation of power to fuel the growth of our nation. Nuclear power will cost us a fraction of the cost of renewable energy, particularly the wasteful plans proposed by the opposition. Nuclear power is cheaper, cleaner, and more consistent than any of the other alternatives, and making the plants government-owned will ensure they are run efficiently and safely. Nuclear power plants are not ugly blots on the landscape like wind turbines nor do they pose the risks we are already seeing in paddocks and paddocks of hideous solar panels. And with the government in charge of building them, we can create jobs, jobs, and more jobs for Australians willing to put in the hard work. Win, win for everyone.

REBECCA: Win for some, but I'm pretty sure not everyone.

Nelson and Jess glare at her. Jake pays no attention to what is going on around him.

JESS: Oh, Mum.

Lights down

Scene 8

The same flat as before. Nelson is sitting in one of the armchairs, playing on his phone. There are baskets of baby clothes scattered around the room. Jess and Rebecca come in - they both look very tired.

JESS: Oh, that was a brutal shift tonight. God, some people are pigs. I can't believe the mess that they leave in some of those offices.

REBECCA: How hard is it to put your rubbish in a rubbish bin that is sitting right next to your desk? Clearly too hard for some assholes. In Mr Waverly's office tonight, there was a mess all over the floor. It looked like he tipped his Chinese takeaway over the carpet and then walked all over it. I was cleaning up Chinese takeaway footprints halfway down the corridor.

JESS: (*to Nelson*) Did Tyrone go to sleep after his bottle tonight?

NELSON: He was colicky as usual but I managed to get him to sleep after walking around and around the table a million bloody times.

JESS: (*laughingly*) I suspect that getting Tyrone to sleep is just about as much physical labour as it was cleaning offices tonight.

NELSON: You can laugh, but at least when you're cleaning offices, you are not getting a headache from his ear-splitting cries.

REBECCA: (*placatingly*) Putting that curtain over the end of the hallway and moving him out of your bedroom has helped him sleep a bit longer at night, though, hasn't it?

JESS: Yes, I think so. At least I am not getting woken with the snuffling sounds he makes all night.

REBECCA: It's funny, isn't it? All of us living here together again? Who would have thought when we sold mum's house and moved here that we would all have to squeeze into this one-bedroom flat a few years later.

JESS: I still feel guilty kicking you out of the bedroom.

REBECCA: It makes better sense. I can easily sleep on a mattress on the floor. There is only one of me.

JESS: I can't believe dad has been gone for over a year now. It was such a shock when it happened.

REBECCA: I didn't realise how depressed he was getting, and I think being unable to finish the one and only cleaning shift he tried was the last straw for him.

JESS: We were all so worried when we got home from our shift that night and he wasn't here.

NELSON: And the police wouldn't take a missing person's report. They said he had to be missing for at least 24 hours.

REBECCA: They found him before that 24 hours was up.

JESS: It was a bit hard to miss him – he was on the ground at the foot of that tall office building in Spencer Street. I hope his death was relatively quick, jumping off the roof.

REBECCA: Poor Jake. He never really came to terms with losing his job and not being able to find something else that he could do with his health limitations.

PETER SAMUELSON: My administration is committed to improving mental health services. We have developed a road map to eliminate the tragedies of substance use disorders and suicides. We will address the negative impacts of COVID lockdowns.

NELSON: (*grumpily*) Well, I'm going to head off to bed. I have an early start in the morning if I'm going to get Mr. Jackson's car ready for him. There's still a fair bit to finish, and I couldn't stay late tonight because you two were starting your shift earlier.

JESS: I guess the one advantage of winter is that it gets dark earlier, and people tend to leave their offices earlier, so we can start cleaning earlier.

NELSON: (*grumpy*) It certainly makes it tight for me to finish the jobs of the day and get the business closed up in time to get home for Tyrone (*he leaves*). I just can't get staff and doing it all on my own is really hard.

REBECCA: (*placatingly*) It's tough on all of us.

Nelson stomps out – not listening to them.

JESS: You're not kidding. Working two jobs and finding time to express milk for Tyrone for the night shifts, and looking after him while I'm trying to work during the day is a challenge. I don't think I have ever felt as tired as I do these days.

REBECCA: You need to look after yourself love. Perhaps you should be taking a supplement some extra vitamins, some iron tablets.

JESS: I'm alright, mum. Things have to get better, right? These are hard times, and you know the old saying: "When the going gets tough, the tough get going." We've been promised better times. They have to come soon.

REBECCA: I don't know about that. Did you hear the news tonight? That report about Martin Gurney? (*sarcastically*) Our esteemed member of parliament.

JESS: Yes, I did hear something. He was arrested, wasn't he?

REBECCA: That's right. Accused of molesting a schoolgirl.

JESS: You're kidding!

REBECCA: No, I'm not. Apparently, it happened at that big event they had last month where he was the guest speaker. She went up to talk to him after the speech and says he took her into another room and molested her.

JESS: Oh, the poor girl. It's courageous of her to come forward. She's not going to have an easy time of it.

REBECCA: For sure. I've heard that he's an absolute sleaze. There was that incident at the youth awards.

JESS: Oh yeah. But that never came to anything, did it?

REBECCA: I certainly haven't heard anything, but you never know what is going on behind closed doors.

JESS: True. Though he probably bought his way out of it.

REBECCA: What's the bet that other women will come out of the woodwork now that it's gone public?

JESS: Not going to take that bet. For sure.

PETER SAMUELSON: I met the Deputy Leader of the Opposition at an official dinner last night. What a crazy, crying low-life. She could never be Prime Minister of this wonderful country. Her yapping in parliament would be a tragedy. You know, all you young men, you have got to push back against these bimbos. You admit culpability then you are dead. You have got to be strong. You have got to be aggressive. You have to push back hard and deny, deny, deny. Let's face it. That big, fat pig can't even satisfy her husband, so he left her for another man, so how can you expect her to satisfy Australia?

Lights down

Scene 9

The scene opens onto the same living area in the flat, but instead of baby clothes scattered everywhere, there are now toys scattered all over the place. There is a washing basket full of laundry sitting on the table with some spilling out. Nelson is sitting sprawled in one of the lounge chairs. There are a number of empty beer cans on the coffee table beside him and one on the floor by his chair. As the lights come up, Nelson takes a swig out of the can in his hand, then looks at it in disgust and throws it down on the floor beside his chair. He is drunk. Off stage, we hear Jess.

JESS: Ow, shit, that hurts, ow ow!

Jess enters, hopping. She is wearing socks but no shoes.

JESS: There's Lego all over the kitchen floor. Why the hell didn't you pick it up when you put Tyrone to bed? Ow ow!

She hops over to the other lounge room chair and sits down, rubbing her foot.

NELSON: Stop your bitching. You ought to try staying home with the little shit all day. It's not easy.

JESS: Nobody said it was going to be easy but you're not pulling your weight. Mum and I are at work at the factory all day and we don't finish till after the last bus leaves town so we have to walk home. The last thing we need is to have to do all the housework when we get back.

NELSON: Looking after the kid is a full-time job. I don't have time to do anything else. You have no idea what it's like being stuck in here all day.

JESS: There are plenty of things you can do to get out with Tyrone. The library has several kids' sessions a week, and Tyrone is always happy to run around in the local park.

NELSON: And what am I supposed to do while he's playing around? Sit there like a stunned mullet?

JESS: There must be other parents you can talk to.

NELSON: All toffee-nosed gits.

JESS: You are not the only father doing full-time child care. There is that playgroup for fathers in Wembley Street.

NELSON: I'm not spending time with those wankers. All they can talk about is their bloody kids.

JESS: Well, what do you expect them to talk about? Their kids are why they are there! You need to make an effort.

NELSON: (*angrily*) Don't tell me what to do.

JESS: If you'd rather, I'd be happy to give it a go. You get a job at the factory, and I'll stay home with Tyrone.

PATER SAMUELSON: We need to protect our children from left-wing gender insanity. Girls need to be girls, and boys need to be boys, and there is nothing in between. And don't get me started on the right way to be a father. A man does not do a woman's job. A woman looks after the home and the kids. That is not a man's job. There are a lot of women who demand their husbands help out with the children and act like a wife. That is just not me. Dads don't play with their kids or change their dirty nappies. I may not see my kids very often, but I'm a great father. I'm a great father, and my kids love me.

NELSON: (*angrily*) Fuck off. I'm not working in a factory

JESS: Well, you're going to have to get a job somewhere soon. You're drinking the last of the money left from selling the garage and tools. Once that is gone, there will be no more beer money.

NELSON: And if I DID get a job who's going to look after the little brat then? We can't afford child care.

PETER SAMUELSON: We need to make child care more affordable. My administration will remove the unnecessary qualification requirements for childcare workers. Why on earth should these workers be required to have a degree? Any woman can look after little kids. They don't need a degree for that. We don't require degrees to become mothers, so why do we require them to look after other people's kids? If we remove the qualification requirements, then we can have more people working in care, and the cost for parents will plummet. Yes, absolutely plummet. And that will benefit the economy. More workers, less unemployment. Better for everyone. Stop making your kids an excuse. Put them in care and get out there and work.

JESS: Mum and I have talked about it. One of us can go back to the night cleaning job, so between us, there will be someone home to be with Tyrone.

NELSON: (*sarcastically*) So you and your mum have got it all worked out, huh? You don't need me at all.

JESS: Don't be silly. Of course, we do

NELSON: Yeah, right. (*He struggles to his feet and waves his way toward the door*) Now you're home, I'm going to go out and see something other than this crappy flat and talk to blokes more interesting than your whiney kid. (*He leaves, and there is a sound of a door slamming.*)

Jess shrugs, and Rebecca enters carrying two mugs of tea.

REBECCA: There you are, love; put your feet up and relax. (*She sits down in the other chair and then notices all the beer cans.*) Oh dear, he's been at it again. Where did he go this time?

JESS: I don't know. Is the pub still open?

REBECCA: It's only 8 o'clock so I guess so. I picked up all the Lego and put it in the bucket. I was talking to Natalie tonight and she had a great idea. She made a big bag out of an old sheet - she threaded string through it and she makes her kids play with their Lego on the sheet so that when it's time to clean up all she has to do is pull the drawstring and they're all tucked up neatly into this big bag.

JESS: I think we have a couple of old sheets - ones where the bottom sheet had worn out, and we were mixing and matching pairs. We'll have to make sure we don't end up with an odd sheet, though – we need pairs.

REBECCA: I'll have a look later and see what I can find.

There is silence for a minute or so as both women sip their tea and relax.

JESS: What are we going to do about Nelson? I don't know what he gets up to all day, but I'm starting to see some things in Tyrone that worry me.

REBECCA: He told me the other day I was a stupid fucking cow. I couldn't believe my ears.

JESS: His language is not the best I know and yesterday when I asked him to pick up his toys, he yelled no and hit me.

REBECCA: It's not good, is it? Do you think he's copying what's happening to him during the day?

JESS: I'm certainly beginning to wonder about that. How about I contact Marilyn at the cleaning firm and see if she can put me on a full-time night shift?

REBECCA: I think you are close to getting a supervisor's position at the factory, and it would be a pity to risk that. Why don't I go back to the cleaning job, and then I can look after Tyrone during the day?

JESS: That's a big ask, mum.

REBECCA: If you could stay on the late morning shift at the factory then I can sleep from 3am when I get home from cleaning until 9:30 am. Leaving home at 9:30 will get you to work in plenty of time and then then you are home by 8 pm in time for me to start at 8:30.

JESS: You're talking as if Nelson is not in the picture at all.

REBECCA: Jess, it's time to face up to it. He's a lost cause. He has drunk nearly all of the little bit of money he got from the sale of the building and plant from his business. I know how devastated he was to lose the family business, but I am not prepared to support him anymore. Your father invested all the money from the sale of your Nan's house into his business and what have we got from it? Absolutely nothing. Money down the drain. Enough is enough. It's got to stop.

JESS: (*a long pause before she speaks, reluctantly*) Yeah, I think you're right.

REBECCA: (*stands up and begins to pick up the toys*) It's not going to be easy.

JESS: (*goes to the table and begins to fold the washing.*) You're right there.

There is a pause while both women focus on what they are doing.

JESS: What makes you think I'm in line for a supervisor job?

REBECCA: I've been watching the manager when he comes in, and he keeps looking at you. According to Nat, Jim, the supervisor on the early morning shift, is retiring, and I know the supervisor on our shift is keen to swap to the early morning shift. Apparently, he wants to finish in time to look after his children after school.

JESS: Well, the extra money would certainly help though I never thought that my life's ambition would be to work as a supervisor in a factory.

REBECCA: I'm not sure the pay increase is very much, but every little bit counts.

PETER SAMUELSON: I love women. Let's face it: I truly love women. But there are many who have to pull their socks up. They come whining to me over every little thing that upsets them. So what if a colleague grabs their pussy? They need to learn to accept it as the compliment it is. And if they can't play in the big pool, then they need to get out and go home. Fix up their own little pools in their own backyards and stop trying to play with the big boys.

JESS: Have you heard they are setting up a community garden down at the old tennis courts?

REBECCA: What's a community garden?

JESS: The idea is that if you go and do some work there, you can take home some of the vegetables they grow.

REBECCA: When would we ever get time to go and work in a garden?

JESS: I was thinking that I could take Tyrone down on a Saturday morning and we could do a couple of hours. It would probably do us both good to get out in the fresh air and I would love Tyrone to have some experience of gardening.

REBECCA: Some fresh vegetables would be a nice change. Did you see the community kitchen advertising free meals on Friday night?

JESS: Yes, I saw that, but you have to go down and line up.

REBECCA: I wonder how many would be left by the time we get there after work? What time do you reckon we could get there by - 745?

JESS: I don't know, but my friend Beryl was going to go down this week, so I can ask her after she's been what she thinks.

REBECCA: She wouldn't be able to pick up a couple for us, would she?

JESS: I think they only give to the people who are there in person, but I can ask her.

PETER SAMUELSON: Yes, I know that the recent inquiry identified supermarkets are price gouging but that is not illegal. The lawyers advise me that this is not illegal. And, I don't agree that putting some kind of regulatory body overseeing them is a good idea. Our country is based on the principle of open market competition, so why should we limit businesses from doing business? Clearly, people are still buying food. If they were not, then the market would disappear, and prices would have to go down. Don't blame the government if your food purchases serve to keep food prices high.

Rebecca has finished picking up the toys. She's put them all in a basket which she stores under the Dining Room table. She stretches.

REBECCA: I'm going to have a quick shower and then get my bed organised. Are you alright to finish up here love?

JESS: Sure, I won't be long. Be careful where you put your mattress. You don't want Nelson falling on top of you again as he did the other night.

REBECCA: Yes, I've thought about that. I think if I push the table over against the wall, I can fit my mattress in beside it and that is well out of the path from the door to your bedroom.

JESS: Are you sure you don't want the bed tonight, mum?

REBECCA: Absolutely not. The last thing I want is Nelson collapsing beside me at some point in the night. The smell of stale beer turns my stomach.

JESS: Mine too. Good night, mum.

REBECCA: Night love. (*she exits*)

Rebecca stands for a moment with some of the washing partly folded in her hands before the lights go down.

Scene 10

PETER SAMUELSON: Good evening, my fellow Australians. I have thought long and hard about what I need to say to you tonight to explain the very difficult decisions that I have had to make. Please rest assured that my decisions focus on what is best for you, my fellow citizens and friends. The past 6 years have proved very difficult. The economic recovery we SHOULD have experienced has been blocked in so many ways. The opposition is only focused on what is good for them and not what is good for the country. We are still seeing the rich getting richer, and our ordinary, everyday families, who are the backbone of our nation, continue to struggle. Every measure I have introduced to parliament to improve things for regular, Australians, for YOU, has been blocked. Fake truths and misrepresentations abound everywhere you look. The left-wing newspapers are happy to report every lie they can find. The media is a huge problem. They report fake news. Liars, cheaters, fraudsters, and imposters run the media and the parliament. Something has to be done. We need to expel these liars and cheats. Get out! You're fired! You're destroying our country. Get the hell out of here! I will not let you use our system to further your own interests any longer. I am going to stop you, and the only way to stop you is to dismantle the system. Dismantle our parliament and create a new form of democracy. A democracy for regular, everyday Australians. Not a democracy corrupted by the left-wing media and all the associated liars, cheats, and fraudsters.

Australians'r'us is a truly democratic party. We will continue to run this country because we have the best interests of our nation in our hearts. We will dismantle parliament, and those opposition liars, cheaters, and fraudsters are from tonight out of a job. I say to them: get out of Canberra, go back to your homes and get a real job, and work for your living. There is no place for you here in Parliament or in Canberra. We will not hold the general election that is due this year. Nor will we have one next year. We need time to repair the damage done by these fraudsters. We need time to build a new system, a truly democratic system that cares about ordinary Australians. I will continue to work for you to build an Australia we can all be proud of. An Australia, where there are jobs for everyone, where everyone who works hard can get ahead, and where our children have a secure future. As your President, your leader, I am going to overturn the wrongs of the past, the left-wing fantasies, and I am going to set our country's footsteps onto the right path. I am going to shape our future. Our vision of democracy will set us on the right path for a glorious future and I will take you there. This is your President signing off for the night. Goodnight, my friends, and rest safe in your trust in me. All will be well.

THE END

The Flag

June 2022

Synopsis

It's not always easy to please the boss and when you are in a hurry everything goes wrong. The idea for this play came from a friend's story about their relationship with their boss.

Characters

* **MARY/MARTY** - female/male of any age

* **PETA/PETER** - female/male any age

* **JAN** - female/male any age

The set is an office with 2 desks, each with a computer/laptop, one at least with a cord running across the floor, 2 office chairs preferably with wheels.

The backdrop shows a large clock with time set at 4.59.

P rushes into a room where M and J are sitting at desks working on their computers.

PETER/PETA: Where do I get a flag? I have to get a flag now.

MARY/MARTY: Huh, flag? What are you on about?

PETER/PETA: The boss told me to get a flag. Now!

MARY/MARTY: What does he want a flag for?

PETER/PETA: Oh, there is some bigwig coming from overseas…

MARY/MARTY: So?

PETER/PETA: He wants to give him a gift and some idiot told him that an Australian flag would be a great gift.

JAN: Really? A flag? Seems pretty stupid to me.

MARY/MARTY: A flag, huh? I dunno.

JAN: Yeah, I reckon a flag is pretty dumb. What about an Australian tea towel?

MARY/MARTY: Or macadamia nuts?

JAN: Tim Tams.

MARY/MARTY: Vegemite.

PETER/PETA: Come on, you need to help me. Where can I get a flag?

MARY/MARTY: Well, if I wanted a flag, I guess I'd look on eBay. You can get pretty much anything on eBay.

PETER/PETA: But I need it for first thing tomorrow morning. I can't wait for it to be posted to me.

MARY/MARTY: Well, I dunno. Have you tried asking Mr Google?

PETER/PETA: Yeah, I suppose that might help. Where's your computer?

MARY/MARTY: Why mine? Why can't you use yours?

PETER/PETA: Because I'MARY/MARTY in your office, dummy. Here, move over.

PETER/PETA shoves MARY/MARTY, and the wheeled chair rolls over and crashes into Jan, sitting at the next desk.

JAN: Hey, watch what you're doing.

Jan grabs a folder of paper and swings at MARY/MARTY. Papers fly all over the floor. MARY/MARTY ducks

JAN: Now look at what you made me do.

JAN begins to pick up the papers whilst MARY/MARTY remains on her chair but wheels herself back towards her desk, running over some of the papers.

JAN: Come on, move out of the way.

JAN tugs at a paper stuck under the chair wheel and tears it.

JAN: Oh bloody hell, now I'll have to reprint this.

JAN turns back to the desk and frantically works at the keyboard. Meanwhile, PETER/PETA is frantically trying to work on MARY/MARTY's computer.

PETER/PETA: Mary/Marty, it's frozen. I can't get it to work. Come and do something.

MARY/MARTY: You idiot! What have you done? I had an open document. You better not have messed that up.

MARY/MARTY pushes PETER/PETA away and taps on her keyboard

MARY/MARTY: It is frozen. I'll have to turn it on and off again. Damn you!

MARY/MARTY switches the computer off and then on again and leans back in his/her chair. JAN gets up and leaves then returns with some papers retrieved from the printer.

MARY/MARTY: If my file is lost, I'MARY/MARTY going to kill you!

PETER/PETA leans over her, looking at the screen.

PETER/PETA: Oh no, it's updating something. You've got to be kidding. Come on, you stupid thing!

MARY/MARTY: Always the way; when you are in a hurry, it seems to know.

PETER/PETA goes over to JAN

PETER/PETA: Can I search on yours? Pleeeeeease. The shops will shut soon and I HAVE to get this tonight.

JAN: No, go away. I have an urgent job to finish, and I'MARY/MARTY already late because you tore my papers.

PETER/PETA: I didn't tear them. You did.

JAN: I don't care. Now piss off!

PETER/PETA: Please, Jan. I'll owe you. Please, please, please.

JAN: Oh, look at the grovel. Grovel again, Pete.

PETER/PETA: Please, Jan. The boss will kill me if I don't get him what he wants. Please, Jan!

MARY/MARTY: Oh, you have him/her at your mercy, Jan.

PETER/PETA: Stop mucking around, you two. This is important.

JAN: Important for you, maybe, not for me. I don't give a shit if the boss is pissed off at you.

MARY/MARTY: It's rather funny, actually.

PETER/PETA: It's NOT funny!

PETER/PETA tries to lean over Jan to get close to her computer but ends up pushing her aside a little, which tangles the cord and unplugs the computer.

JAN: Well, look at that. You've turned it all off. Just as well I had finished what I was doing. Perhaps that is fate telling me that it's time I went home.

PETER/PETA: Hey, I can use your computer, right?

PETER/PETA plugs it back in, and it fires up. While it is starting, Jan collects her handbag and gets ready to leave.

PETER/PETA: Jan, what is this? Have you got a password on this?

JAN: Well, yes, the screensaver works independent of whoever is logged in.

PETER/PETA: What is it?

JAN: What is what?

PETER/PETA: Your screensaver password. Come on, Jan.

JAN: Here, move out of the way.

JAN leans over and types in the password whilst making sure PETER/PETA cannot see what she is typing. PETER/PETA tries to peek but JAN manoeuvres to hide what she is typing.

JAN: Okay, you are in. I'MARY/MARTY off. Bye, all.

JAN exits

PETER/PETA leans anxiously over the screen, waiting for it to load.

PETER/PETA: You are kidding me! Not again!

MARY/MARTY rolls over in her chair and looks at the screen.

MARY/MARTY: Oh, the same update. You know that IT scheduled these for 5 pm on the assumption that we will all be going home by then.

PETER/PETA sits with head in hands. MARY/MARTY rolls back to her computer

MARY/MARTY: Well, mine is still updating. I'MARY/MARTY going to leave it running and get going. Goodnight Pete.

MARY/MARTY gathers her handbag and coat and leaves

PETER/PETA jiggles in the chair, tapping hands/fingers, jiggling legs, and mutters

PETER/PETA: come on …… hurry up …….. come on, you stupid thing ……. Oh god, look at the time ……. Come on …….

Lights fade

Backdrop flashes to the words "The next day" with a clock showing 10 am, then back to the office backdrop.

MARY/MARTY and PETER/PETA are sitting at their computers working as before. PETER/PETA comes in slowly.

JAN: Hey PETER/PETA. Did you get what you wanted last night?

MARY/MARTY: Oh yes, the flag. I gather you used Mr Google on Jan's machine – it was still running this morning.

PETER/PETA: It took 30 minutes for the updates to load and then the machine turned itself off and on again. I didn't have your password, Jan, so I tried yours, Mary/Marty.

MARY/MARTY: Oh really, and why not go into your own office and use yours?

PETER/PETA: Mine was with IT being reformatted. It took overnight to do. I only just got it back.

JAN: Why, what did you do? Click on one of those shonky links?

PETER/PETA: The email said it was from my bank. It looked legit.

MARY/MARTY: Well, you are an idiot! You should know not to fall for any of those scams.

JAN: Did IT find any viruses?

PETER/PETA: They didn't even try – they just wiped everything and started again. I've got to put in all my personal settings now. It's a real pain!

MARY/MARTY: So, did you find your flag?

PETER/PETA: Yeees …. Sort of.

JAN: What do you mean sort of?

PETER/PETA Well by the time I could ask Mr Google, the shops were all shut except for the supermarket.

MARY/MARTY: You won't find an Australian flag at the supermarket, you dork.

PETER/PETA: Well, I sort of did.

JAN: What do you mean?

PETER/PETA pulls out of her/his pocket (or from behind her/his back) a cocktail stick with a tiny paper flag.

MARY/MARTY and JAN stare at it and then begin to giggle.

Lights down. From offstage in the black comes the boss' voice, as loud as possible

BOSS: Where is that fucking idiot Peta/Peter?

185

THE END

Waiting Room

June 2024

Synopsis

Appearances can be deceptive and we cannot judge people on our first impressions.

Characters

- SAINT PAT – waiting room administrator – any age, any gender

- BRENDA – female, any age

- DOG – any age, gender

- TANYA – a prostitute

There is a sign saying "Gateway" with an arrow pointing offstage left. There is a bus parked stage right. SAINT PAT is sitting at a desk writing. BRENDA enters and strides up to the desk. BRENDA is dressed conservatively and stylishly. SAINT PAT does not acknowledge BRENDA, who begins to tap her foot in annoyance, clear her throat, etc. Finally, she speaks:

BRENDA: Hey, you.

SAINT PAT: (*looks up after a pause*) Me?

BRENDA: Yes, you. I am waiting.

SAINT PAT: Yes, I see that you are (*s/he lowers her/his head and continues to write*)

BRENDA: *(snatches the paper)* So do something about it then. I'm waiting

SAINT PAT takes another piece of paper and begins to write again.

BRENDA: Oh, for god's sake *(she crumples the paper without looking at it and throws it on the floor, then turns away and strides over to the sign)*

SAINT PAT: (*quietly and to herself*) Yes indeed, that is so *(and continues writing)*

BRENDA strides off in the direction the sign is pointing. As she moves offstage DOG rushes in and bumps her. BRENDA shrieks and stumbles back, then pushes past DOG and exits. DOG runs over to SAINT PAT, and SAINT PAT pats her/him.

SAINT PAT: Well, what do you think?

DOG barks and runs in a circle. The barks sound like the word 'no' over and over again.

SAINT PAT: No? She's certainly an impatient one, but her record (*she holds up the paper she was writing on*) shows that she did a lot of good in her lifetime.

DOG runs to the crumpled paper, picks it up, and gives it to SAINT PAT. SAINT PAT sighs and opens it up, smooths it out, reads it, and then looks at DOG.

SAINT PAT: There are a lot of good works on this record, DOG. They have to count for something.

DOG shakes her head vigorously and barks, 'no, no, no.'

SAINT PAT: Are you sure? I really hate to send them to the other gate, you know. It can take them decades to work their way back.

DOG runs in a circle and then exits past the gate sign. SAINT PAT writes a little more on the crumpled paper, then puts it in the 'out' tray and selects another paper from her 'in' tray. She begins writing. TANYA enters. She is a prostitute and dressed accordingly. She looks around fearfully, sees SAINT PAT, and sidles up to the desk.

TANYA: Hello

SAINT PAT: (*stops writing and looks up*) Hello.

TANYA: Wot do I do now? Can you tell me? I dunno wot's goin' on.

SAINT PAT: That's okay. Lots of people are confused when they get here. I'm the gatekeeper.

TANYA: Yeah, okay. Gidday (*a pause*). Gatekeepa for wot?

SAINT PAT: Gatekeeper for the Gates of Heaven.

TANYA: 'Eaven. Ya mean that's real?

SAINT PAT: It certainly is.

TANYA: Oim in the shit then, ain't I? 'Ardly been a good Christian girl me.

SAINT PAT: I don't know. Looking at your record here – didn't you take in your friend's daughter when she died in childbirth?

TANYA: Well yeah, but wot else was I gunna do? Foster care ain't for little mites like 'er. I should know.

SAINT PAT: And by all accounts, you gave her a loving home.

TANYA: O'corse. She was a lovely wee thing, and look at 'er now. I'm right proud of 'er, I am.

SAINT PAT: And so you should be. A lawyer, at her age, and doing really well in that neighbourhood law clinic.

TANYA: Yeah, an' she worked too hard. I always tell 'er, you can't win every battle, but she just fights on and on. The bloody man wins too many, ya know.

SAINT PAT: And I see here that you donated a lot of your savings when the centre looked like it would have to close down.

TANYA: Bloody government cutting funding like that. It ain't fair. Those poor sods need all the 'elp they can get.

SAINT PAT: I must say I find it rather amusing that it's money from what one might call immoral pursuits that keeps them going.

TANYA: Hey, them lot might not fink much of my line of work, but it's honest, and I never cheated anyone.

SAINT PAT: No, I can see from your record that you were scrupulously fair.

BRENDA enters and stomps up to the desk. She pushes TANYA aside. TANYA shrugs and steps back. DOG accompanies her and runs in circles around the 2 women. TANYA pats DOG

BRENDA: The gate will not open.

SAINT PAT: No, you need a pass.

BRENDA: Well, give me one then (*she reaches to snatch the paper SAINT PAT is working on – SAINT PAT holds it out of her way and carefully folds it into quarters. She looks around BRENDA to TANYA*)

SAINT PAT: TANYA dear, here is your pass. The gate is over there (*she/he gestures to the sign*)

DOG jumps up, grabs the paper from SAINT PAT, and runs to TANYA. TANYA laughs and pats DOG

BRENDA: That disgusting mut (*she aims a kick at DOG that DOG easily avoids*)

TANYA: Hey, that's not nice. You are a lovely doggo. Yes, you are a lovely doggo (*she pats DOG. DOG jumps up and down, then grabs TANYA by the hand and begins to drag her to the gate. TANYA laughs and holds back*). But I can wait if this lady wants to go first. There ain't no hurry.

BRENDA: (*sniffs and turns her back on TANYA*) My turn. The pass.

SAINT PAT looks through her out tray and selects the crumpled paper. She reads it. Then she carefully folds it in quarters, marks it with a large black X and passes it to BRENDA. BRENDA looks at the paper, then strides over to DOG and snatches TANYA's paper from her. She looks at it and strides back to SAINT PAT's desk, throwing both onto the desk.

BRENDA: Explain. Why does mine have a black cross and hers does not? What does this mean?

SAINT PAT: TANYA's is a pass through the Gates of Heaven. Yours is a pass for the bus over there (*she gestures to the bus*)

BRENDA: What do you mean a bus? I don't take buses. Those are for people like her. If I want to go anywhere, I take the Rolls.

SAINT PAT: There are no Rolls here. Unless you want to stay in the waiting room forever then I suggest you get on the bus and take a ride.

BRENDA: Oh well, at least you see that I am too good to walk. Not like some

She glares at TANYA and boards the bus. It departs; the sign on the back says, "Destination: Hell."

DOG takes TANYA by the arm and pulls her towards the gate.

SAINT PAT (*looks up and smiles at TANYA and DOG*): Have fun.

SAINT PAT waves and DOG and TANYA disappear.

THE END